Running in the Dark

Rena Cooper

Matador
9 Priory Business Park,
Wistow Road, Kibworth Beauchamp,
Leicestershire. LE8 0RX
Tel: 0116 279 2299
Email: books@troubador.co.uk
Web: www.troubador.co.uk/matador
Twitter: @matadorbooks

ISBN 978 1800462 625

British Library Cataloguing in Publication Data.
A catalogue record for this book is available from the British Library.

Printed and bound in Great Britain by 4edge Limited
Typeset in 11pt Minion Pro by Troubador Publishing Ltd, Leicester, UK

Matador is an imprint of Troubador Publishing Ltd

The book is dedicated to Sam, Jack, Fiona and Aijaz

Contents

Chapter 1

A Beginning

Soon it would be dark. The day was cooler now and drawing to a close, but, even in the fading light, he could see right across the park, over the railway line and into Abercrombie Terrace. The windows, row on row, were black, with the last of the sun's rays reaching only the far side of the buildings. That was the side of the old tenements where the kitchens would be busy, noisy, full of the sounds and smells of evening. At the entrance of the close, stood the solitary figure of PC Bob.

Bob Wishart shifted his weight from one foot to the other and back again. He'd been at his post for what felt like forever, watching, waiting and hoping that his vigil would soon come to an end. It had been a long day and he was beginning to feel cold. It was early summer but the late afternoon had brought an unexpected chill. Now and again, Bob marched up and down in front of the close, scanning the empty terrace, a forlorn sentry on duty, hoping that his quarry would appear at any moment! However, Bob was as sure as he could be that that was not about to happen. The boy had made a run for it. He was convinced of that and where he was now was anybody's guess! There were obvious dangers for a lad on his own. Bob had two sons and right now they were safe at home, where this boy ought to be. First light tomorrow, he'd organise a proper search, get a few of the early shift on the trail. Might even be a few of the local worthies willing to help. Not much more to be done today.

Above PC Bob and slightly to his left, Daniel could see someone else – someone else who was watching, an unfamiliar figure. A woman was standing at the window of the third floor flat, where he and Uncle Barney lived. It was impossible at this distance to see her face, impossible to see who she was but that didn't matter. *Who* she was didn't matter. Daniel was pretty sure he knew *what* she was and why she was there. That made all the difference.

From high in the tree, Daniel could see it all - all that he needed to see - and, if he turned his head, just a little, he could see another face at another window just a few yards above and to the right of where PC Wishart now stood and stamped. This face belonged to Esther. Daniel suspected hat she would know exactly where he would be, even though he hadn't known that himself until, in the depths of the tunnel, he'd finally run out of breath. He'd climbed this chestnut many times and now, in full leaf, it was just what he needed. He was invisible - but Esther would know. She would know. She seemed to be looking straight at him - a white face in the gathering dark.

Soon, the lamplighter would come just as he did every night at this time. As the summer days grew longer, his times would change but, for now, he still came just after seven o'clock to light the gas lanterns in Abercrombie Terrace. Most of the other parts of Riverside now had brand-new electric streetlights but this part of town was shabby, waiting to be modernised. Uncle Barney had explained it all. Uncle Barney liked the old gaslights and he was in no hurry for things to change. Daniel felt much the same way. He and Uncle Barney agreed on many things. They were good together – or at least they had been until the last few days or even weeks, when things had changed.

There was something in the air, something different that sat between them like a black cloud – a silent something that made him uneasy. It had crept up on them out of nowhere and settled over their evenings together. It had been there for two weeks, although it was difficult to say exactly when it had arrived. He'd tried working that out when he was in bed at night but it was no good. Once or twice he'd caught Uncle Barney just looking at him as if he were about to say something but, when Daniel had met his eye, he'd quickly looked away. Something was brewing but he had no clue as to what that something might be. He'd have to be ready because one day it would pounce. He was sure of that. They would both have to be ready. The dark cloud would have Uncle Barney to deal with and he was "The Best". Daniel would tell them so - if they ever found him - ever asked him. But they wouldn't find him. Not now. For now, he was safe.

He settled down, shifting his position in the fork of the tree so that his legs could stretch out a bit. Pushing his hands deep into his jacket pockets, he leaned back against the rough trunk and looked round to check that his rucksack was firmly hooked on the branch by his side. He would be needing that later but, for now, there would be no moving from this spot even though his legs ached and the cold was beginning to bite. Until the park was empty and shut for the night, this tree was where he would stay.

The park was his world, his and Esther's. Daniel knew Bankside Park. He knew it well. The tenements, grey and forbidding, had no gardens but their children were never short of places to play; the back courts and the old wash-houses gave good cover for chasing and hiding and the street was quiet enough for football. Esther liked to join in with the football but most of the girls preferred to gather in the shelter of the entrances to the closes, happy with their dolls and prams or, when the time was right, sit on the grey stone steps to swap scraps. They had their own games; everything had its season. Skipping would be everywhere for a while and then the chalks would be out and Esther would desert the football team to mark out "beds" on the pavement to play peever. Still, the park, only a short distance away, was the best place to be. Everyone knew that!

When school had closed for the day, the sloping green where the giant tree stood had been full of people, people of all ages: mothers straggling home to make the tea, some with prams and some without; grannies coming back from the shops with string bags of groceries on their arms; old men wandering down from the bowling greens - and children of all ages, running, shouting, even fighting. Now it was quiet, quieter than Daniel had ever known it before. Daniel was also quiet; quiet, watchful and, above all else, like Bob Wishart, increasingly cold. The tweed jacket, snatched up in a flying hurry, was thin and had seen better days. His eyes kept returning to the main pathway, which lay between his tree and the flowerbeds. Beyond this was the main railway line and, to the left, on this side of the railway fence, was the entrance to the tunnel, a dank walkway that passed underneath the line, a place of shadows and echoes, with rusty metal gates at either end.

Soon the parkie would appear. His shrill whistle warned all those who dared to linger that the gates were about to be locked for the night. Time to run, if you knew what was good for you.

There were several gates to Bankside Park and Daniel knew them all, knew where they were and knew the sequence in which they would be locked. More importantly, he knew where to go if you found yourself shut in. He'd been shut in on one memorable occasion, when he'd been climbing trees, but he'd found a gap in the railings where he'd been able to squeeze through. There was always somewhere to go if you'd left things a bit late.

The park gates were tall and topped with spikes. Climbing over was not an option. The park keeper, Duffy, a man hated and feared by all, made it a rule to close the main road gate first, then these two, one at either end of the tunnel, before making his way up the slope that led to the swings so that he could lock the two back gates, which were probably on his way home, although nobody seemed to know exactly where he lived and no-one that Daniel knew would ever be brave enough to ask.

On his way, Duffy, as part of his nightly routine, would pause to lock the ladies' shelter and stop at the playground to chain up the swings and the wooden roundabouts. Every so often, he would give a sharp blast on the whistle he wore around his neck just in case someone had dared to ignore his previous warnings. Should he catch sight of one of these unfortunates, he would soon remind them who was in charge, threatening all sorts of vengeance if they failed to make themselves scarce before he sealed them in for the night. The polis were usually mentioned somewhere in this angry tirade along with several references to the large walking stick that he carried in his left hand. This was usually shaken vigorously high above his head in order to drive home the point that he was not a man to be trifled with. Sometimes, a few curses would be added for effect. Daniel always gave Duffy a wide berth. Trailing behind Duffy was Rustler.

Once upon a time, Rustler must have been a cute and cuddly pup but that was now very hard to imagine. Rustler didn't resemble any other dog that Daniel had ever seen. He appeared to be a terrier of some sort but his sandy coat was always matted and risen in spikes while his distinctive smell was overwhelming, even from a distance, which was, by far, the best place to be when he came into view. His temper, like that of his owner, was short and his teeth very quick to show themselves whenever his lips curled back in a snarl, which was almost his permanent expression. Rustler did not give the impression of being a happy dog and was always ready to share his view of life with as many other living souls as possible. In short, like his master, Rustler was to be avoided.

Daniel didn't have long to wait for the park-keeper to make his entrance. Right on time, Duffy and Rustler rounded the corner by the Memorial Garden. Duffy's eyes swept the empty park as he marched purposefully along the path, a tyrant in his realm. Even in the relative safety of the tree, Daniel stiffened. This was probably the high point of Duffy's day when he could lock everybody out. Daniel suspected that he would ideally like to keep the park to himself and keep it locked up at all times! He'd probably like to shut the gardeners out as well as everybody else! He rattled the doors of the wooden potting sheds as he passed by, just in case one of the gardeners had failed in his duty. Everything had to be locked up tight; there were always gangs of lads about and there was no way that Duffy would leave the park at their mercy. They were troublemakers. He had them in his sights. It seemed to Daniel, when he thought about it, that Duffy had a problem with the human race in general!

The breeze no longer rustled the leaves and the still air carried every sound. A wood pigeon settled on Daniel's branch and then, realising it was not alone, clattered out of the tree in some alarm. Daniel cried out and Rustler turned at once towards the unexpected sound. Baring his teeth and barking furiously, the terrier catapulted himself across the grassy slope, his eyes fixed on the tree. Even at this distance, Daniel could make out the curled lip and bristling rage that always preceded an attack. He didn't have long to wait! At the foot of the tree, the hairy ball of fury rose up on its hind legs, snapping and snarling and clawing at the trunk. Daniel wasn't sure whether the dog could actually see him; the thick canopy of leaves gave good cover, but the dog knew that someone or something was up there and that was enough.

Duffy had decided to check things out and, stick at the ready, was now heading in Daniel's direction. He'd just begun to cross the grass when voices from the woods close to the boating lake caught his attention. Two boys, younger than Daniel, came stumbling into view. They were carrying fishing nets and jam jars with string for handles. Water spilled everywhere as they desperately tried to run without losing their baggy minnows.

"Mr Duff!" they yelled. "Please, Mr Duff, wait for us!"

Rustler, distracted, raced towards the terrified boys. Snapping at their heels, he pursued them all the way to the tunnel entrance and Duffy, with his targets in clear sight, made the most of the moment. Assuming that the boys had been the cause of Rustler's annoyance, he harried them every running step of the way until, with a final wave of his stick, he chased them into the gaping mouth of the tunnel.

It suddenly dawned on Daniel that he had been holding his breath. At last, he felt able to breathe again; Duffy would probably give up once the boys had fled from the tunnel. They would escape at the outer end and run for home through the prefabs. After that, it would take only a few minutes for the parkie to fix the padlock on the iron gate and return to secure the iron gate on this side, within the park itself. It was a nightly ritual, which Daniel had watched many times from the safety of the front window on the third floor of Abercrombie Terrace.

Rustler was the first to emerge as he raced ahead of his owner to escape the confines of the tunnel. Despite his bravado, the tunnel was not Rustler's favourite place. The underground path below the railway line stretched for a mere thirty yards but, despite the glass bricks in the roof, there was a heavy, dank, dripping darkness about the place, especially at this time of the day. The walls ran with water for most of the year; it pooled on the concrete walkway below creating a slippery carpet of moss. At either end, mounted high on the tiled walls were ancient lamps on black brackets but these had long-since ceased to work and no-one had shown any interest in repairing them. They simply added to the gloom. However, the best and the worst experience that the tunnel had to offer was that of being there underground and peering up through the grimy glass at the railway lines above when the trains rushed like fiery dragons just overhead. Some of the glass bricks had fallen away so that the underside of the trains looked almost too close. The children would scream and cover their ears as the steam engines thundered overhead on their way north heading out of Bankside Station. Some people pretended to be scared. Some were scared!

Rustler clearly hated the tunnel and did not enjoy this part of his master's nightly routine. Now that it was over, he was ready for home. By the time Duffy had emerged from the darkness, Rustler was already half-way up the hill that led towards the swings. He'd had enough for one day! Mercifully, Daniel's tree was forgotten.

As the shadows deepened and the birds fell silent, Daniel knew that it was time to go. He rubbed his legs to ease the cramp and, throwing his rucksack down on to the grass below, he lowered himself to the ground. His legs and arms ached from keeping so still for so long and the creeping cold had made things worse.

Despite the long hours in the tree, he had formed little in the way of a plan; everything had happened so fast that it had been impossible to think very clearly beyond the obvious. Now, for the first time in his life, he really was alone and what happened next was up to him.

PC Wishart had finally left for home and Abercrombie Terrace was empty of life. The town would be quiet now. Suppers would have been eaten and cleared away. Radios would be blaring and tin baths settled in front of kitchen fires. Bath time would be well underway at the O'Callaghans by now. One last look. No sign of Esther! Time to go! He knew where he was going and he knew it would be best to be there by nightfall. Clutching his rucksack, Daniel slithered down from the tree and, without a backward glance, he began to run.

Chapter 2

Shadows

Once, when they'd been late coming home from the coal yard, Uncle Barney had told him never to be afraid of the dark, not even the towering darkness of Abercrombie Terrace when the street lamps were left unlit. That had happened frequently since the war. Uncle Barney had often talked about the darkness of the blackout and being a fire watcher. Darkness had been his friend.

"You couldn't see a hand in front of you," Uncle Barney had told him. "Anybody who showed a light soon got a knock on the door and a sharp reminder to draw their curtains."

The bombers had come night after night with the shipyards in their sights, shipyards that had always been the lifeblood of Riverside itself and had become even more important when war came. There could be no guiding lights.

Once, walking home late from a visit to the stables, Uncle Barney had told Daniel to close his eyes tightly in the black dark and then open them slowly so that his eyes could get used to it and pick out landmarks among the shadows. Daniel thought of his uncle's words now as he crossed the park. This was familiar ground and yet, in the fading light, it was a different place. Keeping to the shelter of the trees and bushes as much as he could, he made his way towards the river. The fence near there had several gaps!

The river and the railings were close to the road. It was risky but he'd have to take his chances. He mustn't be seen before he'd even got started, before he'd made a plan, before he'd really had time to think. He needed a plan that would work and that wasn't going to be easy.

From the edge of the woodland, Daniel could see that the large metal gates were shut and padlocked just as he'd known they would be; Duffy had done his work well. What he'd not expected to find, however, was that the gaps in the iron gate, which had been there for several weeks had been repaired! Shiny new metal barred his way! Daniel shook the bars but they didn't move. They were rock solid.

The river was running high; there had been heavy rain for most of the week but the day's sunshine had brought the promise of change. Half-way between the two banks was the stone boat. When the weather improved enough to make it an easier job, the gardeners would wade out and decorate the boat with plants and then people passing through the park gates would stop in wonder to admire the floral boat in all its splendour. The plants were grown in the greenhouses near the railway line. That was where the gardeners worked their magic all year round. They raised all their plants from seed and were pleased when people praised their efforts, neat flowerbeds with colourful patterns of marigolds, geraniums, begonias and giant dahlias. Everything was carefully measured and marked out with pegs and twine as soon as the winter frosts were over. As the seasons changed the park blazed into colour. Every year they did something different.

The planting had been late this year because of hard frosts and recurring rain so the old boat stood bare and forlorn, an empty vessel of cold stone. In the dark, he could just make out the shape of its jagged, grey hull.

Cramming his shoes and socks into his rucksack, Daniel stepped gingerly into the water. It was cold, even at this time of year, so cold that he almost shouted out. Somehow, he managed to choke back a cry. The stones underfoot were sharp and shifted with every step but there could be no turning back. There was mud too and once or twice he felt himself slip and only just managed to keep his balance. The dark was coming but the new electric street lamps on the main roadway provided Daniel with an uninterrupted view of the world beyond the boundary and the far bank of the river. He could pause on the boat and make sure that no-one was on the footpath by the road before heading for the far side. He would have to be careful. The river was shallow here, only up to his knees but the ominous rumble just a few yards to his left was a constant reminder of the need to measure every step.

The main gates straddled a concrete bridge, below which a deep waterfall tumbled and foamed. The drop was around fifteen feet into a churning pool below and, naturally, there were many tales of children being swept away, never to be seen again!

For one week each year, in late autumn, when the days grew short, Bankside Park was opened after dark. Coloured lights were hung everywhere, twinkling in the trees and hiding among the leaves It became a place of wonder and surprise. Ice cream sellers and local businesses took the chance to advertise their wares and make some money and the locals made the most of occasion. The Electricity Board now joined in the fun, setting up a huge marquee to display the very latest things that every home should have. The very latest fires, cookers and even refrigerators were set out for all to see. Not many people could afford to buy anything but they looked all the same. Fridge and cooker doors would be opened and closed and opened and closed again, the interiors examined with longing before they were firmly closed for good - often with a sigh. Maybe next year? Then everyone would drift over to the old Gas Board tent and do the same thing all over again!

"The Illuminations", as this special week was called, were very popular and Daniel and Uncle Barney had a grandstand view of some of it from their own front window in Abercrombie Terrace. However, they had to make a special visit if they wanted to see the waterfall as it was at the opposite end of the park but it was always well worth the trip. The falls were a special feature and were somehow illuminated by lightbulbs hidden behind the descending water. The cascading curtain kept changing colour from moment to moment and there were lots of enthusiastic cries from the assembled crowd as the falls turned pink, blue, red, green and orange in turn. For Daniel, this was the highlight of the show and he would stand rooted to the spot for ages watching the colours playing on the fast-flowing water as it disappeared beneath his feet. These falls, however, frothed and tumbled under the bridge to join a fast-flowing river, which widened as it made its way towards the deep shipping lanes that brought work and wealth to the town.

Daniel, struggling to keep his balance in the cold water, remembered the tales of children being swept to their deaths, carried off by the river, carried out to sea. He had never been sure how much truth there was in these stories but he was not about to take any chances; this was a serious river and, following days of summer rain, it was running high.

Reaching the stone boat was a relief but, after a pause, Daniel had to move on. Soon it would be night. For now, the pathway beyond the far bank was clear. No-one was about - but that could change. With luck, the second half of the crossing would be easier. There would be light from the lamps by the path. He hoped there would be no broken glass in the swirling water below him.

The prefab kids were a tough lot. They often smashed bottles just for fun. They scared Daniel almost as much as the gangs of older boys hanging around the street corners. This was one of their favourite haunts - that and The Crescent - where the ground was still scarred and littered with debris from the air-raids. People said that unexploded bombs from the Blitz still lay hidden in the wreckage of buildings that had once formed an elegant crescent of grand houses, which had been owned by the wealthiest factory owners and businessmen of the town. Daniel, like many other children, had to pass that way each day on the way to and from school. Picking his way through the stones and bricks that had once been mansions held no horror for him; it had become part of life. The piles of rubble were just there, the wreckage of people's lives, lives that were now in pieces just like these buildings where once they had raised their children. Now and then Daniel wondered where they were now but he didn't ask too many questions. It had taken days and weeks to dig out the living and the dead. Some had managed to reach the shelters but not many.

Daniel found it strange and sad that, after all of this, anyone would want to spend their time smashing up even more things but some of them did! Breaking bottles against the railway bridge was a popular but pointless activity, whichever way you looked at it. Apart from anything else, money was short in Bankside and, if you took your empty bottles back to the shop, Sam gave you money for them. It wasn't a fortune - but it was something! Time to move on again. Daniel tested every step as he waded through the swirling water. There were always eddies here because of rocks in the river and the falls to his left but, as a strategy, the slow, cautious approach worked well and, thankfully, he managed to keep his footing all the way to the opposite bank. The mud there almost sent him backwards into the icy river but by grabbing hold of the weeds, he was able to pull himself free. From the knees up, he was dry but below that he was wet and numb with cold.

For a while, he crouched, shivering, among the reeds. He used some of the rough grass by the roadside to wipe the worst of the mud from his feet and legs and took time to scan the main road, up the hill and down. From the safety of the shadows, he had a clear view in both directions. The coast was clear but It was going to be difficult to move without leaving a trail of muddy prints that anyone could follow. He would have to take the chance. Nearly there! There could be no mistakes now.

From his right, a motorbike suddenly roared into view, speeding down the hill towards the main road. Daniel made no move until the noise of its engine had faded. Time to move on! He wouldn't be going far but he paused just long enough to put his shoes and socks back on again. His legs and feet were still damp but that wouldn't have to matter.

Sam McAllister's shop was only a few yards from the iron gates of the park and it would be in darkness now, except for the lamp at the side that shone out over the yard by the garages. He would have to run for it there, just for a bit. He'd keep tight to the wall and make for the shadows.

A group of girls from the council houses came into view. They went giggling past, heading in the direction of the town. Their high heels clacked on the pavement as they made for the tram stop. More waiting! But not for long!

When the tram trundled off, its lights disappearing as it rattled over the brow of the hill, Daniel made his move.

Looking neither to right nor left, he ran as fast as he could manage with legs that were so cold he could hardly believe they existed any more, towards the first door in the row of crumbling garages. The key was safe and ready in his pocket so it didn't take long to undo the padlock and squeeze himself between the heavy wooden doors. It only took moments and then the familiar smell of engine oil and old leather told him he was safe – at least for now! He closed the door and locked it behind him.

They would be looking for him by now and by first light the search would begin in earnest. By then he would have to have a plan but by then he would have to be gone!

Mr Morgan and his pals, most of them well into their seventies, gathered every day at the garages. It was where they went to smoke their pipes and talk about old times. There, they'd talk about the old days, days spent in the shipyard and the factory and about the war and old friends. Most of their lives had been spent building ships or sewing machines! Now they used their skills on cars and motor car engines. Many happy hours were spent working on or talking about the treasured vehicles that were their pride and joy. Cars were washed; cars were polished; car engines were dismantled; car engines were re-assembled; engine parts were soaked in paraffin and now and again the cars were actually driven somewhere – usually not for very far as petrol was still expensive.

Each garage had its own character according to the personality and preferences of its owner. Some were tidier than others. Mr Morgan's was perfection in that respect. The garage shelves, made from bits of timber rescued from old packing crates, were lined with jam jars full of screws and nails of all sizes, pots of grease, rusty biscuit tins full of nuts and bolts, spanners of all sizes, used matchsticks and, of course, oily rags. In short, all you could possibly wish for! To the untrained eye it was a collection of assorted rubbish but to Mr Morgan it was Heaven! This was where he felt most at home.

Mr Morgan was older than Uncle Barney but he was a good friend, all the same. Daniel loved to sit and listen to the old boys talking and, now and then, he'd chip in with a question or two about how things used to be. He'd been accepted as an honorary old boy and welcomed, whenever he rolled up, to join in with the garage gossip. Sometimes, he was allowed to help with the work on one of the cars. He was learning things, useful things about engines and he was even beginning to think that one day he might learn to be a proper engineer. One afternoon, Mr Morgan had presented Daniel with his own key to the garage so that he could let himself in if he arrived before the rest of the gang. Mr Morgan trusted him and Daniel liked that.

Mr Morgan liked to talk but he was also a good listener. Uncle Barney was a good listener but he didn't say much. After a few drinks, he would let himself go a bit and then he could be funny, the life and soul of the party – but usually he melted into the background. He was a good man but Daniel knew him well enough to know when something was brewing – something was brewing now and it didn't feel like something good!

Uncle Barney was OK. That was something that the American soldiers had said; "OK!" It had sounded good. Daniel had added it to his vocabulary. All the GIs were gone now. Some had stayed for quite a while in Abercrombie Terrace. They'd been popular visitors. They were always laughing and joining in with the street games, kicking the can around or playing football in the back courts. They brought chocolate and comics, even lemons for Mrs Morgan. She could make a good lemon tart! The Americans were gone now – but everyone still said, "OK."

Safe in this familiar place, Daniel could think, sort out what to do next, think through what had happened and try to make some sense of it. On sunny days, with the doors wide open, the garage was warm and welcoming. Now there was a chill in the musty air and, in a corner, somewhere at the very edge of his hearing, something scuttled for cover, something small, something of the night, something in the shadows that was even more afraid than Daniel himself.

The car was unlocked. Mr Morgan always kept it that way, with the brake off and a brick behind the rear wheel. He had explained to Daniel that he did that so that the car could be pushed out quickly if a fire broke out. Mr Morgan thought of everything! His Standard Ten, with its wide running boards, was his pride and joy. Every Sunday, he would take Mrs Morgan out for a ride – but only if the sun were shining! Rain meant that the trip would have to be put off for another day. The car might get wet!

The back seat was piled with cushions and rugs just in case, riding in style on the rear bench, Mrs Morgan should feel cold along the way. Daniel was glad of the rugs. He drew a particularly thick blanket around his shivering frame and hoped that Mrs Morgan wouldn't notice any tell-tale traces of mud left behind. He reached into his rucksack for his torch. He would have to risk a small light so that he could see to eat his bread and cheese as well as one of the wrinkled apples he'd stuffed into his jacket pocket at the very last minute. He would have been glad of a drink but there had been no time to organise that. Maybe tomorrow. He did have some money - not much - but something to fall back on. He'd remembered the cracked teapot on the mantel where Uncle Barney always kept the shillings for the gas meter. He hadn't taken all the money but he still felt guilty about the coins he'd hastily stuffed into his trouser pocket. It felt like stealing.

There wasn't a great deal of cash about in Abercrombie Terrace. Uncle Barney was a good worker and earned steady money but they couldn't afford many treats. There were outings to town now and then and Daniel always had proper shoes. There was always food on the table and Daniel didn't have to queue up at school for tickets for free dinners like some of the children had to do. He was one of the lucky ones.

In the black dark of the dusty garage, Daniel didn't feel lucky and yet he'd been able to escape the clutches of PC Bob, not to mention the woman at the window! Perhaps he had been lucky after all – but would his luck hold? The night, for now, was his friend but tomorrow, in the daylight, things might not be so easy. He closed his eyes tightly then opened them again very slowly, peering into the darkness and tried hard to convince himself that, by morning, he would have a plan, a plan that would work!

Chapter 3

Alone

The day had been very long and sleep had been slow in coming. When it had, it had been fitful, disturbed by unfamiliar sounds and dreams in which he was lost and cold and trying to find his way back to Abercrombie Terrace. It was an uncomfortable, restless sleep that ended with the first pale shafts of morning light. The sunlight, as it struggled through the tiny windows high above him, formed faint, flickering patches on the dusty floor and walls. It was time to go – time to be on his way!

There was no-one about as Daniel slipped unseen into the yard. There was, as yet, no heat in the sun and he shivered as he locked the door. Pocketing the key, he headed for cover in the safety of the trees behind the shop. He wouldn't be able to make much progress until evening came but that would give him time to think. It was Friday now. He had to remember that. He had to keep on remembering what day it was and, somehow, what time it was. He didn't have a watch so there would have to be other ways of working things out. The sun was low. By mid-day, when the sun would be high in the sky, he hoped he'd have a plan of some kind but, for now, his only idea was to keep moving and keep out of sight.

On reaching the lane, he spotted the man. He was walking slowly, with a canvas bag over his arm. As he came nearer, Daniel could see that the bag was full of wood. He'd seen this man before. He was from the prefabs. He must have been collecting firewood and not wanting to be seen. Just like Daniel, he must have made an early start, keen to get home before the shipyard workers turned out for the early shifts. Daniel kept to the edge of the path beyond the hedge and tried not to breathe. The man was very close now. He would only need to turn his head and Daniel would be in his line of sight. The bag suddenly slipped and the man paused to grasp it with his other hand. He tried dragging it behind him but it just flopped to one side and the wood tumbled out. It was heavy and it was unwieldy but the kindling was needed to keep his family warm so he was not about to give up. Daniel kept absolutely still, not daring to move an inch. As he watched, the man scraped the wood back into a bundle, grumbling to himself, and pressed the firewood down to make it more secure. Finally, with difficulty, he went on his way, trailing his awkward bundle beside him as best he could. Daniel breathed a sigh of relief.

It had been a close call that had shown just how easy it would be to give himself away. However, as he began to make his watchful way along the lane once again, a plan of sorts began to take shape in his mind, a plan that might even work but for it to have a chance of working he had to make sure that no-one saw him, that no-one took him back to where PC Bob was waiting, that no-one took him back to Abercrombie Terrace and the woman in the window. He had decided! Somehow, he had to reach Billy. Billy would know what to do. He'd thought about Mr Morgan but had decided against it. Mr Morgan gave good advice but it was mainly about engines. Billy would know just what to do. After all, Billy had Ina so, if all else failed, Ina would know exactly what to do. Ina always knew!

Moving faster now as his limbs began to warm up, Daniel made for the copse. He'd hidden there before - but just for fun. This time it was different! The golf course was always quiet during the week with only a few old men to worry about. Uncle Barney had once explained to him that it was a "municipal" course, which meant that you didn't have to be rich to play there. Uncle Barney didn't play golf but he'd worked there for a while as a green keeper. The war had left the course peppered with craters and Uncle Barney had helped to put things right. It had taken months of hard work but Uncle Barney had been glad of the money. Uncle Barney had explained that, after the raids on the town, the enemy fighter planes often emptied their bomb racks as they headed for home. The golf course had taken several hits.

The shipyards had been the main targets as well as the ordnance factory where the tanks were built and tested - "Churchills" and "Centurions". The town was proud of its record. However, a heavy price had been paid. It had taken a hammering but the shipyards and the factories had escaped the worst of the bombing. Somehow, the workers had kept going night and day to meet their vital deadlines and keep the ships rolling off the slips. Riverside and Bankside had done their bit for the war effort and their citizens were rightly proud of that – but many people had been lost and most of the buildings bore the tell-tale scars left by the Blitz, when the town had burned for days. Whole families had been wiped out and Daniel's own mother and his grandparents had been killed in one of the last of the air raids.

Uncle Barney had enjoyed working on the golf course. That was more than could be said for all of his jobs over the years. At the present time, he was working for Mr Gilligan, the coal man. He loved that. Some of his time was spent in the office, which he said was boring, but the best bit was that Mr Gilligan still kept horses and ponies for pulling the coal carts. Some of the milkmen in the city still used their old horses but most coal merchants had got rid of theirs and changed over to motorised trucks. Uncle Barney wasn't interested in trucks but looking after all the horses and ponies gave him pleasure. He knew every animal by name and they all knew him. One of the local lads, Paul Fairley, helped him. Paul walked with a limp and sometimes struggled to find work but Mr Gilligan had taken him in and said that Paul was one of his best workers. Uncle Barney liked Paul and had taken him under his wing. Daniel liked him too.

Trees were things that the golfers worked hard to avoid. If golf balls landed in the copse, they were unlikely ever to be seen again. Lost balls were given up as hopeless! That would serve Daniel well. He raced across the fairway and threw himself among the moss and bracken that thrived in the cool, damp darkness under the trees. Tree-climbing was Daniel's thing but there should be no need for that. With luck, he'd be able to wait here until it was dark and eat some of his meagre rations while he waited. He still had some food left. Not much! There was some bread and a piece of dry cheese, one more apple and a piece of fruit cake that Mrs O'Callaghan had given to Uncle Barney for them both to share. In view of the fact that Uncle Barney was now in a prison cell, Daniel felt no guilt about having it all. He hadn't realised how hungry he was until he started to eat. The cake soon disappeared, as well as the bread and cheese. He finished up with the apple and kept a couple of biscuits for later. He would have to find a way of getting something to drink; his mouth was parched and the apple had been dry. He wondered what the food was like where his uncle was. Sadly, Uncle Barney would now be finding that out at first hand!

The sun rose higher in the sky and even here, in the shade of the trees, Daniel began to feel warm and a little drowsy. Sleep was catching up with him but he fought it. He needed to think and this was as good a place as any. He could see clearly for some distance on every side and, as he'd expected, no-one was about. There was no possibility of anyone approaching unseen. He would spot them long before they were near enough to be a problem. To his left was a tall lime tree. It was an easy climb and, if necessary, Daniel would be up there like a shot! It was that or run for it. One or the other! He had a breathing space!

Yesterday had been Thursday! He reminded himself of the day. It had begun just like any other Thursday with Uncle Barney waking him five minutes before seven o'clock to tell him to get ready for school. He'd got washed and dressed in the kitchen just as usual because it was always warmer there. Uncle Barney had been busy making toast as he normally did and the warmth from the grill was always welcome; the tenements were cold in the mornings, even in summer. After his breakfast, Uncle Barney had set off at about eight o'clock, as he did every weekday. Daniel had finished his breakfast - as well as his homework for Miss Deacon - and set off for school.

It was a short walk along Abercrombie Terrace, past the prefabs - Daniel always ran here - and across the wilderness that was The Crescent. Some of the ragged children had stopped to pick handfuls of the dandelions and coltsfoot that were growing among the debris and they'd shouted to Daniel as he'd raced past. One boy had waved something above his head, shouting that he'd found a grenade. Perhaps he had but Daniel wasn't inclined to stop and find out. Sometimes people did find things left over from the raids. They'd had a talk about it at school. Miss Deacon had told them all what to do if they found anything that looked suspicious. Waving it above your head and wailing had not been on her list of sensible options!

The steep steps that led up to the road were always a challenge. How fast could he run up them without stopping? There were no railings to hold on to as they had long since been removed for their metal. Uncle Barney had said it was for the war effort. Sometimes, just for a change, Daniel would run up the wide stone balustrades that still retained the stumps of the railings poking up through the stonework, ready to trip the unwary! He'd excelled himself on the balustrade and so he'd been in high spirits on reaching the main road at the top where he always paused to check for traffic before crossing to the other side and he'd done that, just as always, before dawdling down the lane that led to Bankside School. He'd been in good time, in fact, a little early.

Once inside the gates, he'd joined in a game that had involved kicking a burst ball about, while listening to Esther chattering on about what they would all be doing at the weekend. Esther O'Callaghan came from a large family, mainly girls. The O'Callaghan clan had swelled to fill a very small flat further along Abercrombie Terrace from Daniel and Uncle Barney. How Daniel envied them! They were a real family, a proper family. There was always something going on at Mrs O'Callaghan's. Mr O'Callaghan was seldom seen as he was a welder in the shipyard and worked very long hours; there were many mouths to feed so Mr O'Callaghan took as much overtime as he could get. A big order for the yard meant that times were good and at the moment Cunard had a liner on the stocks. Orders didn't come much bigger than that! It meant that the O'Callaghans had proper shoes this summer instead of welly boots.

It amused Daniel that all the children in Esther's large family had been named after people from The Bible, with the only boy in the family being called Joshua. Despite her determined efforts to keep her army of six children clean and tidy, Mrs O'Callaghan did not appear to be able to keep her charges free from the head lice that were the curse of Bankside School. As a result, one or other of the tribe was regularly sent home, almost on a daily basis, to have the pink soap and fine tooth comb treatment. Of course, in school, no-one wanted to sit next to an O'Callaghan no matter which class they were in! The biblical names appeared to offer no protection, which seemed a shame. It was widely circulated by children and parents alike that the nits were carried by the O'Callaghans, who seemed to be permanently scratching their heads. Daniel had had nits many times. Uncle Barney didn't seem to mind much. He'd notice Daniel scratching his head and, with a sigh, would fetch the fine-tooth comb and a sheet of newspaper so that the hunt could begin! Daniel nearly always sat next to Esther, unless they were separated for talking too much. Esther was Daniel's best friend.

It had been almost at the end of lunchtime that Esther had delivered her bombshell! The morning had passed without incident. Apart from the fact that two O'Callaghans had been sent home instead of one, everything had been quiet and orderly. Miss Deacon, herself, had been in a particularly good mood as everyone had remembered to bring their homework in on time - something of a record - and no-one had spilled any milk at playtime or complained about the crates having been left too close to the radiators - also, something of a record. New carbolic, pink and firm, had appeared in the outside toilet block, instead of the old and rather slimy scraps of soap, which had become so unpleasant that no-one wanted to wash their hands at all. The janitor, Mr Craig, had warned everyone within earshot that the new soap was to last for at least two weeks as his stocks were running low. He always said that! Probably, all jannies said that. It was probably in the rule book for jannies in training! It had been a fairly good day at Bankside. Then things had changed, at least as far as Daniel had been concerned!

The O'Callaghan family all had free dinners but not Esther, who always went home instead. She said that it was because she was a fussy eater but Daniel felt sure that it was really because of the scary and rather disgusting things that some of the more creative thinkers said about the food! It put her off! Also - perhaps the main reason - she hated standing in the dinner queue and having to hold out her yellow free dinner ticket. He'd never heard of anyone saying anything unkind but Daniel knew that she minded a lot about people knowing that her family had to have free meals. Daniel always enjoyed his school dinners. He was pretty sure that, at times, he qualified for free dinners too but Uncle Barney "never got round to filling in the form" so Daniel paid for his dinner and that was that. Inside himself, he was glad.

The meals weren't bad and certainly as good as Uncle Barney's cooking. He'd finished his rice pudding and eaten Edward Simpson's as well because Eddie didn't like milk pudding of any kind even with jam in the middle!

Before afternoon lessons had begun, they'd all gone out into the playground for a kick about when, out of the blue, Esther had come tearing through the gates. Esther was no runner but it was clear that she must have raced all the way from Abercrombie Terrace; her face had been bright red and you could tell that she'd been crying. Esther never cried!

When, finally, Esther had found her voice, she had struggled. The words had tumbled out between gasps, jumbling one into the other, which had made it difficult for Daniel to make sense of anything she was saying. He'd had to tell her to slow down and say it all again.

"It's your Uncle Barney. He's been in a fight! I couldn't hear it all. They were talking on the landing. I just ran! He's got into some trouble down by the canal and they've taken him away in the polis van! The Welfare Lady's coming for you. Mum told PC Bob that you could come in with us but he said it wasn't up to him and we've too many children already. PC Bob said they'd got it all fixed up and you were to go to a big house in the country while things got sorted out. I know what that'll be. It'll be the children's home, Daniel. Percival House! You mustn't go there. It's awful." Esther's face had been streaked with tears.

Daniel had taken Esther by the arm and dragged her towards the children's shelter to escape from all the flapping ears. One or two eager eavesdroppers had managed to pick up a few scraps of information and had edged closer to find out more but a warning look from Daniel had told them to keep their distance, that this was important and not for them! Grudgingly, they had sidled off in the direction of the school building to await the imminent ringing of the afternoon bell.

Despite the fact that the story had been very confused, it had been quite clear to Daniel that this was no time for delay. As far as he'd been able to work out, although it had been difficult to piece things together through Esther's sobs, Uncle Barney had been in some trouble that morning, some serious trouble to do with the lads from the prefabs, something to do with a fight and "Bible Billy". Uncle Barney must have been in the wrong place at the wrong time - or the right place, depending on your view of things, and, somehow, he must have lost his temper. According to Esther, a boy had ended up in the canal and now Uncle Barney had been taken away in the Maria. Esther had listened to PC Bob from behind the kitchen door before making a dash for it through the back courts when Mrs. O'Callaghan had returned to dealing with two wriggling children. Mrs O'Callaghan had been busy at her post on the shared landing in the close, attacking head lice with the fine tooth comb, working energetically on the two O'Callaghans who'd been sent home from school. While they had wriggled and protested, PC Wishart, on his usual beat, had been intent on saying as little as he could get away with about what had happened while keeping himself at a safe distance from the nits, or "jumpers" as he insisted on calling them.

Esther hadn't been able to hear as much as she would have liked but she had been able to make out that Daniel was to be collected at the end of the school day. The woman from The Welfare was to collect him after school.

The Welfare had been given Uncle Barney's key so that she could take Daniel home after school and help him to pack some things before she took him to wherever he was to go. PC Bob was going to make sure that the school knew exactly what was happening and Mrs O'Callaghan was to keep an eye on the flat while it was empty. It had all been agreed!

The Welfare took orphan children to Percival House, the children's home on the far side of the river. Esther had often described in lurid detail the horrors of Percival House. She'd heard all about the poor children who'd had to go there because their mothers were dead or beat them with sticks or were too drunk to look after them any more! Esther had painted a very gloomy picture indeed. Daniel wasn't sure how much of it was true but, in the end, he'd decided not to take any chances. Percival House was not for him!

According to Esther, it had been decided that Daniel could not be left at Abercrombie Terrace on his own because he was only eleven! According to Esther, her mum had tried to persuade PC Wishart that Daniel would be safe in her care. (Bob's knowledge of the overcrowding that already existed in the tiny flat and his first-hand observation of the scratching children had suggested otherwise.) In any case, he'd said that it had all been arranged and couldn't be changed. It seemed that Uncle Barney had asked PC Bob Wishart to keep the O'Callaghans in the picture as they were his friends, his and Daniel's. (Having done his duty, PC Wishart had been anxious to be on his way. Despite the fact that he'd kept his distance from the wrigglers, children AND nits, he'd had a feeling that his head was beginning to itch. Mrs Wishart was not going to be pleased!)

Esther had made a run for it. Daniel had to be warned. He would know what to do. Esther was sure of that. But, in that headlong flight along Abercrombie Terrace in the direction of Bankside School, she'd had no glimpse of an idea. No ideas or plans had come into view and, by the time she had reached Daniel, all that had remained was panic – and Esther was one of the calmest people he'd ever known!

Daniel had known at once what to do. He'd taken to his heels and run for it! He'd run as fast as he could go, out of the school gate, down The Crescent stairs over the waste ground that was all that was left of The Crescent itself, past the prefabs and along Abercrombie Terrace. His flight had, amazingly, gone unnoticed. The streets and the close had been quiet, almost empty of people. Everything had been on his side. His house key always hung around his neck. He'd had it ready! Once inside the flat, he'd wasted no time. Some food, a little money from the teapot on the mantelpiece and a few clothes and bits and pieces crammed into his rucksack. Not too heavy! He'd almost forgotten his torch, had dashed back for it and then, after locking he door, he'd made his escape down the stairs, looking neither to right nor left, his feet flying down the stone staircase. Mrs Ritchie had been hanging out some washing in the back court, which meant a roundabout path behind the wash-houses to avoid her sharp eyes but then - no-one - and a free run along the back alley that led back to Abercrombie Terrace itself. Not until he'd cleared the tunnel and settled himself high in the tree had Daniel felt safe. There, far above the ground, in one of the tallest trees in Bankside Park, he'd known that he was out of sight. In the safety of its branches, heavy with leaves, he'd given himself some time to think and make his plans. One thing had been uppermost in his mind. He was not going to Percival House and that was final! Luckily, Abercrombie Terrace had been completely deserted and the vast chestnut, his own special tree, had been there, of course, as if waiting for him. He'd climbed it many times. Waiting had been easy. Waiting was something he was good at. Waiting was what he was doing now, here in the copse. He could not, however, wait for long. He needed to be on his way.

It was still and quiet here in the shelter of the trees, with hardly a breath of wind. Minute by minute, time was passing. Insects droned in the undergrowth and, inch by inch, the shadows lengthened. A group of distant golfers idled across the fairway, their voices faint and indistinguishable in this seemingly endless landscape. Faint birdsong drifted from somewhere high in the depths of the wood and the summer air was heavy with the lingering scent of new-mown grass. Tucking his rucksack under his head, Daniel drew his jacket around him and closed his eyes. Curled up in a ball, he fell asleep.

Chapter 4

New Ground

Someone laughing! The sound awakened him. They were close, only a few yards away - a couple, holding hands and laughing as they crossed the wooden bridge to the pathway that ran alongside the burn. Daniel turned his head away, not wanting to be a spy, and yet that's what he was now – someone on the edge of things, outside and looking in but it was safer that way, at least for now. The couple disappeared down the lane, their voices fading, and Daniel looked around him. He wondered what time it was but, now that he was alone again, he knew it must be time move on. The sun was low in the sky, which told him that he'd been asleep for far too long. Late afternoon, then, but too long to wait for evening.

However, as he gathered his belongings together, Daniel realised that he was not alone, not quite. Off to his right, just beyond the fringes of the copse, a solitary, stooped figure was scouring the hedgerow, rifling through the leaves and grass cuttings that had gathered there. Daniel recognised him. Tramps very often came this way and this one was a regular visitor to the town. He was known by many names but the one that came to mind was, "Devil O'Neill". There would be no going anywhere, not for now! Daniel kept very still.

All the children kept clear of O'Neill and frightened each other with tales of his evil doings. It was unlikely the scare stories were true but it was best to play safe. The Devil, despite his rags and permanently thick layer of grime, always seemed to have money to spend, mostly on whisky, and Daniel had often wondered how he came by it. Now he knew where at least some of it was acquired! Over his arm, O'Neill carried a large, frayed canvas sack, into which, now and again, he dropped something foraged from the long grass. Intrigued, Daniel strained to see more. Golf balls! Golf balls gone astray! The clicks, as they clattered into the bag, told Daniel that there were many similar trophies already hidden there. Devil O'Neill would be more than happy to sell them back to their grateful owners at bargain prices and make a bit of whisky money in the process. Daniel settled back into his hiding place and watched the slowly disappearing figure with some relief. As he shuffled out of sight over the brow of the hill, The Devil stopped, just for a moment, to drink from a bottle that he took from the torn pocket of his trailing mackintosh. It made Daniel realise how thirsty he was, himself. He couldn't remember when he'd last had a drink. His lips were dry and his tongue was sticking to the roof of his mouth but there was no time to worry about that. He had to move on.

The sun was low and Daniel needed to leave but now there was another problem. On Fridays - and he'd forgotten that this was Friday - the end of the week – the course could be busy later in the day. Peering out between the trees, he spotted a small group of players drifting in his direction. Their voices carried on the wind and they were growing louder as they approached. What if they did see him! He was just a boy walking! A boy on his way home, perhaps! Could be anyone! He was just a boy, an ordinary boy with a rucksack! As long as he kept close to the hedge, he should be safe. By now, though, people would be searching for him. People would know there was a missing boy! He might have to run but his legs felt like lead and, as he looked up at the hill in front of him, he didn't relish the thought of making a dash for it. Still, he would have to take his chance!

Keeping to the hedgerow, Daniel made slow progress towards the road, which he could just make out beyond the boundary fence of the course. This would be new territory, somewhere that he'd never been before and, for that reason, he would have to be on his guard. It would be unlikely that anyone would know him here but there was always the worrying possibility that he might be noticed by someone who was nosey enough to ask who he was and what he was up to. There was always somebody!

Daniel knew of several in Abercrombie Terrace and had a feeling that they were everywhere, busy-bodies, probably members of some conspiracy of nosiness that had followed on from the wartime duties of being fire-watchers or something! Close to home, everyone knew him. "That's Daniel Abercrombie," they would say. "It was his father who jumped on to the line. A brave man. Dreadful business!" Remarks such as these were often accompanied by whispered asides as the story was retold. Daniel always tried his best not to hear.

The world at the top of the hill and beyond the perimeter fence was not what Daniel had expected, The houses here were very different from Abercrombie Terrace. Each one was large and not joined to its neighbour. Each house had its own garden with its own garden path leading up to its own front door and its own fence or stone wall to mark it out as separate from the next. The stones were grey like the scattered remnants of The Crescent where he walked to school every day but here there was no sign of chaos or destruction. The gardens were large and green, with tidy lawns and neat flower beds. There were no tenements or back courts here, no brick wash-houses or old wally closes to be seen. This was a very different world from the one that Daniel and Uncle Barney knew. Two of the houses had cars parked outside them – not like the old cars that belonged to Mr Morgan and his pals. Quite the opposite! These were very large and shiny limousines parked proudly on broad gravel drives and glinting in the dying rays of the sun.

All the houses had windows upstairs as well as downstairs except for one. Right at the end of the row, was a long rambling bungalow with all its rooms at ground floor level. The larger houses looked smart and lived-in but this one was different. It had an air of neglect. The rusty gate lay back on its hinges and the curving path was dusty and unswept; the peeling green paint on the door of the porch was faded by the sun and every window was dark, with shabby curtains drawn shut against the light. Daniel's gaze, however, was drawn to an outbuilding that sat some distance from the house itself. It was a small weather-worn summer house. Made of sun-bleached timber, and with faded blinds at the windows, it had seen better days but next to it, just to one side, was a stand-pipe with a brass tap. Daniel waited no longer. Within a few strides, he was there. A patched, rubber hose was roughly taped to the spout as if ready to water the strange plants that grew all around. Daniel removed this with some difficulty but it was worth the trouble. The water, when it came, was surprisingly cool and refreshing. Just what he needed! He hadn't known that plain tap water could taste so good.

When he had drunk his fill, Daniel looked around him. This was the oddest garden he had ever seen. Here, at the side of the bungalow, a wide lawn sloped towards the roadway, bordered by strange plants of every shape, size and colour. It was bewildering to the eye. There weren't many flowers but there were several spreading green palms with leaves like dinner plates and spiky clumps of brown and red fronds spearing through matted undergrowth. It made him think of the jungle. Stretching skywards, in the centre of the lawn and much taller than the bungalow, stood a towering Monkey

Puzzle Tree! With its stiff, brush-like branches, it formed an eerie silhouette against the sky.

It was so dark that it was almost black. Daniel had seen a tree like this once before. In fact, it was the only familiar plant in this entire garden. Once, when they had made a rare visit to the city, Uncle Barney had shown him such a tree in the Botanic Gardens. He had touched one bristly branch and then he'd understood the reason for its name. Each spike, stiff and sharp, would present a challenge to any climber and, being a climber himself, he had sympathised with the monkeys! Uncle Barney had said that it was "exotic". Daniel had liked that word and now, more than ever, he appreciated its meaning.

The sound of someone approaching prompted Daniel to crouch down behind the summer house. The footsteps drew nearer and Devil O'Neill shuffled into view. He must have turned back on himself for some reason. O'Neill stopped to stare in Daniel's general direction but, fortunately, didn't linger. Muttering to himself, he quickened his step and hurtled off down the hill. His evenings were usually spent in town in the heady atmosphere of Drummond's Bar. It looked as if he could be heading in that direction now although Daniel couldn't be sure. This was new ground. Following The Devil was a possibility but just considering the idea made Daniel shiver. No way! Besides, it was still too light to be able to follow him unseen. Better to be lost. He'd been lost before. He'd be all right.

The latch on the summer house door was crude and rusty but it moved easily enough for Daniel to slip inside. There was a dusty warmth within that was not unwelcome. A wobbly, metal table and a battered basket chair were the only items of any size, although, as well as these larger items, the clutter did include a pile of old books and magazines, some discarded sweet papers and several empty seed packets. Shards of broken plant pots and a scattering of earth littered the floor. On the table, Daniel noticed an old map of Africa, spread out and weighted down with stones. Some of the place names had been heavily underlined in pencil. Perhaps, Africa was where this gardener had found his inspiration. Because of the dirty windows, the light inside the summer house was poor and it was almost impossible to read anything properly. Daniel tried to work out some of the place names on the faded map but, in the end, he had to give up.

Checking that the back door of the bungalow was clearly in sight and making himself as comfortable as possible in the battered, wicker chair, Daniel settled down to wait for nightfall. Safe for now, he could take time to finish what was left of his dwindling food supplies. In addition, he could make use of the water supply. That was a bonus!

Suddenly, without warning, and for the very first time since he'd set out from Abercrombie Terrace the day before, a tear rolled down Daniel's face, and then another and another until there was a constant stream. In the empty summer house, where no-one could see, where no-one could hear, he covered his face with one of Uncle Barney's best handkerchiefs and he cried.

Uncle Barney had once said that it was fine for boys to cry if they needed to. Daniel hadn't cried when his family had been lost– not at first; he'd been too young to understand what had happened, too young to realise that they'd gone for ever, that, despite all his longings, they would not be coming back. It had taken him some time to realise that, like his father, they would not be part of his life any more except in his dreams and in the stories told to him by Uncle Barney. His father had died the year before when he'd tried to save the tiny boy on the line. The accident had happened very near to the station. Uncle Barney, his dad's younger brother, had looked after Daniel following the air raid that had taken his mother and his grandparents and had adopted him as his own. They'd been together ever since. There were some distant relatives north of Crianlarich, but Daniel didn't know who they were – and he didn't need to know. He was happy with Uncle Barney.

Daniel and Uncle Barney lived in the house that had belonged to Daniel's grandparents. Uncle Barney always referred to the flat as "the family home" as if it were something really grand. It wasn't. There was a kitchen, which was also the living room, two bedrooms and a bathroom. Not all the flats in the street had a proper bathroom with a big bath so at least that was grand if nothing else was! Uncle Barney had given Daniel a home, when he needed one, and given him a bedroom of his own. What would happen now if Uncle Barney had to go to prison? Daniel had no answer and so he cried. He cried for both of them, for Uncle Barney and for himself. He wept for all that had been lost and could never be found again. He wept for his father and for the tiny boy lost on the line.

As the sun began to set and the sky turned pink, he dried his eyes and stuffed the wet handkerchief into his trouser pocket. Then, looking around to make sure that no-one was about and checking that his rucksack was securely fastened, Daniel prepared to move on. Devil O'Neill had taken a downward path, a steep roadway that would probably lead back into town. It should be safe to make a start. He would head in that direction. Slowly and quietly he opened the door and stepped out into the cool air. Before leaving, he paused for one final mouthful of water from the tap then turned towards the gateway. As he did so, he noticed a thin sliver of light escaping from one of the windows. The curtains were not quite closed, making it just possible to see into the room beyond. It proved irresistible. Keeping low and clutching his bag in his right hand, Daniel crept forward until, with one final stretch, he could reach the window sill. Despite the grime on the glass, he could see that someone was sitting close by the fireplace. There was no fire in the grate but the figure appeared to be hunched over it as if hoping to find some comfort there.

A crackling sound revealed that the man was, in fact, attempting to tune a battered old wireless that stood on a table close to his armchair. Even at this distance, there was something familiar about this person that Daniel couldn't quite explain.

As he moved closer to get a better view, the gravel crunched beneath his feet. It was a small sound - but it was enough. Like lightning, a face appeared at the window, nosing the curtains aside. Not a human face this but a face that Daniel instantly recognised. A ball of snarling teeth and temper hurled itself against the window. Rustler! With a cry, Duffy was on his feet and heading towards the door.

The slope was just enough to hasten Daniel's flight and more than enough to make it difficult for Duffy to follow at any speed. In this half-light it would not be possible for him to be sure of his quarry but Rustler was keen to find his mark. Twice those snapping jaws came close to Daniel's flying ankles but, each time, a swipe of the dangling rucksack sent him rolling. By midway down the hill, the terrier had given up and, with one final, half-hearted bark, he scuttled back to his master. A raging Duffy shouted something but, thankfully, it was impossible to make out what it was. Curses, no doubt. Fury at having been disturbed in his jungle lair! Daniel was free. He just had to hope that he would be able to stop running before he reached the road at the foot of the hill. It was a close thing! The roadway wound down through unfamiliar streets of neat houses and past a small wooden church. There were very few people about and those who were to be seen were too preoccupied with their own business to take much notice of a boy on his own. Excellent! Duffy was now more of a mystery than ever but he would have to remain so for the present – perhaps forever!

As he rounded the bend beyond the church, Daniel felt he could relax a little. It was the back of the park. He knew this place but he had always viewed it from the other side of the fence. This side was out of bounds to Daniel on his own, according to Uncle Barney, who had very few rules but insisted on strict observance of the ones he did have! Still, Daniel now knew where he was. Familiar ground once more. Keeping close to the high, black railings of Bankside Park, he edged his way towards the main road. In the shadows of the trees, he was confident that he would be difficult to identify in the fading light but, beyond the side streets, he would have to be careful. If anyone did happen to recognise him, he would just have to run for it; there would be no alternative. Crossing the road, he saw a friend of Uncle Barney's heading up the hill from the canal. An open gateway gave him cover until the danger had passed.

Finally, with relief, Daniel realised that he was almost there! Any minute now he would be within sight of the swing bridge and "The Wayside Pulpit". A few minutes more and he would be there! His legs ached and his stomach felt cold and empty but soon he would be with Ina and Billy. Soon he would be sitting by the stove in their old caravan and all would be well. Ina and Billy would know what to do. They would know what had really happened to Uncle Barney and, even more important than that, they would be certain to know how to help Daniel to get him out of wherever he was now and get him home again. Everything was going to be all right.

A few more steps and the famous blackboard that stood next to the footpath came into view. Everyone for miles around knew it as The Wayside Pulpit. Everyone who walked past Ina and Billy's painted van would pause on their way to see what Billy's daily message had to offer. Copper-plate writing would carry a message from the scriptures. Some of the children from Daniel's class would laugh when they saw it. Sometimes, they would throw things in the general direction of the board or try to reach over the fence to rub out some of the letters. This often meant that Billy's message became unreadable or was transformed into something rude, which made the laughter even louder. For some reason, making fun of Bible Billy was a popular pastime with some of the locals – and not all of these were children. Daniel had never been able to understand why. Billy was a good person who would help anyone and Ina was just the same but lots of local people avoided them and seemed to regard them as outsiders. Not Uncle Barney! Whenever he was worried about something, Uncle Barney would talk things over with Ina and Billy in the reassuring warmth of their caravan. They were like family, helping to make up for the family that had been lost. Uncle Barney had mended their caravan when it had let the rain in and had helped Billy dig out his tiny vegetable patch.

Daniel stopped dead at the edge of the pavement and stared. In the spot where Ina and Billy's brightly painted caravan normally stood, there were only charred timbers and a wind-blown scattering of ash. Their precious garden, which they'd planted alongside the towpath was now a wasteland, devoid of life. The acrid smell of smoke lingered in the air and there was something else – the unmistakable smell of petrol! Of Ina and Billy, there was no sign. All that remained was a simple, shining message in white chalk on the blackboard. Its wording, in Billy's elegant hand, was clear for all to see: "God is Love".

Chapter 5

The Road to Glenderrin

Drummond's Bar, a few streets away from the swing bridge, was a popular meeting place but it was not for the faint-hearted. Before long, as Daniel well knew, its customers would be drifting out on to the pavement, full of whisky, rum and beer. Often, fights would break out over nothing at all and fists and bottles would fly until the polis, never far away at closing time, arrived to take charge and load some of the worst offenders into the maria. Restoring order often involved a few heads being cracked as batons were drawn and for some a long night in the cells usually followed! It was a weekly ritual.

In his hiding place, pressed against the wall of the close right next to the public bar, Daniel listened. He needed to find out what had happened to Billy and Ina and he had a feeling that this was the place to be, the place where local news would get an airing. Here, safely out of sight of the doorway of the public bar, all he had to do was wait and listen.

From inside Drummond's the sounds and smells of the evening seeped out into the night; someone inside had brought a mouth organ, providing a tuneless accompaniment to whatever else was going on. Only men were allowed into this bar, men who would soon be spilling out on to the narrow pavement with tongues loosened by whisky and in no hurry to head for home.

Women were banned from Drummond's Bar with its sawdust covered floor and spittoons in every corner but, in the glow of the orange neon light that lit the pavement outside, several wives would be lying in wait, hoping that not all of Friday's wages had disappeared into the landlord's eager till.

Some wives preferred to send their oldest sons to waylay their errant fathers as they emerged from the smoke-filled bar. Not an easy mission - and many a lad received a thick ear for his pains.

Daniel waited for what seemed like an eternity. There was a chill in the close that contrasted unhappily with the imagined warmth of Drummond's Bar. At last, the doors flew open. The Devil O'Neill - and others - poured out as they did every Friday night at this very hour. Gathering on the pavement, they would linger in each other's cordial company for as long as it took for the landlord or someone in uniform to move them on.

Daniel edged as close as he dared; he was about a yard from the pavement and did not want to go any further.

He strained his ears for any mention of what might have happened to Ina, Billy or Uncle Barney and he didn't have to wait for long!

The Devil was in full flood. He was a regular visitor to Billy and Ina's caravan. Ina had taken him under her wing, which meant that he was never short of a hot cup of soup or a cast-off jacket to keep him warm on his travels. Ina had knitted scarves and mittens for him although she would never ever give him money. She knew exactly what he would have done with that!

Over the din, Daniel was able to gather that O'Neill was extremely put out! He had planned on making a call at Billy's caravan earlier in the evening but had stumbled upon the same devastation that Daniel had found. Now, with a drink inside him, he was raging and full of threats about what he would do to those responsible for setting light to the one place where he'd known he could safely expect a warm welcome. He was demanding to know everything there was to know about the burnt-out shell by the roadside. It was clear that several members of the group had already tried to explain the situation to the best of their ability but had failed to make him understand. Daniel was in luck. One inebriate, with more patience than the rest, made a final effort to penetrate the dark recesses of the old man's brain. It was an uphill struggle.

Flattening himself against the tiled wall of the close and keeping in the shadows, Daniel listened and slowly began to piece together the bare bones of the story. The arrival of two young constables on the beat, however, brought the proceedings to a sudden halt. They were assisted by several young lads, not much older than Daniel himself. Several angry wives had indeed sent their reluctant sons to collect their long-awaited fathers. Gradually, the pavement cleared and the night was finally still. The landlord locked his doors and settled down to count the takings. It had been a profitable evening. Paydays always were.

Leaning back against the cold tiles, Daniel turned the story over in his mind. There were obvious gaps but a vague picture had begun to form. The events of the day before were beginning to make more sense. He had been able to learn that, early on Thursday morning, a gang of the local lads had decided to have some fun at Billy's expense. The Wayside Pulpit was a regular target for the corner boys so Billy and Ina were used to being the focus of their frustrations. However, something much more serious than the usual pranks and name-calling had resulted in Billy and Ina's caravan being set alight. Petrol had been thrown. Made almost entirely from wood, the caravan and its rickety, makeshift extension had very rapidly been consumed by the quickening flames, burning easily in the dry air, with thick clouds of black smoke drawing the attention of passers-by on their way to work. It sounded as if Uncle Barney, on his way to the coal yard, hadn't waited to ask questions but had launched himself at the nearest culprit, who had, as a direct result, found himself in the murky waters of Bankside Canal. Just as Esther had reported, Uncle Barney, for his pains, was now in the hands of the local polis, driven off in the maria. Fortunately, Ina and Billy had escaped the flames and, for their own safety, had been moved, with their dog, Alfie, to a safe place in the country. They had lost almost everything they owned.

"Glenderrin?" The Devil had seemed particularly annoyed to learn Ina and Billy's destination! "I was past there only yesterday," he'd shouted after the dispersing crowd, "and I'm not headed that way again until next week. Old Colonel McPhee, he'll have 'em. He'll have the minister and his missus. He'll see 'em all right. He hates those hooligans. Won't have 'em on his place. Shoots at 'em with that shotgun of his! Reckon he's killed more layabouts than the blasted Gerries ever did. You need to keep well clear of old McPhee. He's cracked!" From his response, it was evident that 'The Devil' had had first-hand experience of Colonel McPhee and his shotgun!

Muttering under his breath, O'Neill had headed off towards the Salvation Army hostel in Ship Lane, no doubt hoping to find a bed for the night. Holding an invisible rifle aloft, he had given a very lifelike impression of a madman wildly shooting hooligans! Clearly, the aforementioned Colonel McPhee!

Esther's story had been right and, with Uncle Barney in the cells, Daniel was pretty sure that, but for her timely warning, he would now be stuck in Percival House. There was nothing to be done for Uncle Barney at this time of night and not much that he could do on his own, in any case, but where was he to go? He shivered at the thought of a night out in the open but he couldn't risk going back to Abercrombie Terrace.

One good thing that could be said in favour of the children's home was that it would have warm beds with sheets, blankets and proper pillows. For a mad moment, Daniel thought of handing himself in at the Salvation Army hostel but he soon abandoned that idea. There was another possibility, a plan that might work.

Once, when Uncle Barney had been delivering coal for Mr Gilligan, he'd taken Daniel with him just for the ride. They'd gone to Glenderrin. With luck, even in the dark, he should be able to remember the way. Daniel was good at places. Geography was his favourite subject at school; he loved drawing maps and colouring them in with the pencils Uncle Barney had given him last Christmas. He would find Glenderrin. That's what he would do! He would find Billy and Ina then, together, they could see what could be done to rescue Uncle Barney from the cells. The burned out shell of the caravan was a different matter. Daniel feared that that was beyond mending.

Outside in the street it was now dark. Daniel realised how hungry he was. Emptiness had crept up on him and now it gnawed at his insides, a feeling made worse by the smell of cooking from the fish and chip shop on the corner. A poke of chips? No chance! He couldn't risk being seen so close to home. He would make his way through the back courts and head for the hills that lay beyond The Boulevard. It would be a long trek and awkward in the dark but with every step he would be moving closer to Billy and Ina. That thought would have to keep him going. Uncle Barney was going to need help. On his own, Daniel knew that he could do very little but, if he could find Ina and Billy, he wouldn't be on his own any more and things would be different. Then, when they'd rescued Uncle

Barney, they would all have to find a way to sort things out at the canal. Without their caravan, Ina and Billy would be homeless. Daniel didn't even want to think about that. "God is Love," he said to himself - out loud. That was what Billy had left as his final message on The Wayside Pulpit. Just like Billy to leave a final message! "God is Love," he repeated out loud. He hoped against hope that Billy had got that right.

Settling his rucksack on his shoulders and turning his collar up to ward off the cool night air, Daniel, silently, made his way between the brick wash-houses, avoiding lights from the tenement windows. Keeping to the shadows, he turned towards the wide road that led out of the town. Keeping close to the walls of the buildings, he would be sure to see anyone before he was seen. The gas lamps provided occasional pools of yellow light but, as he left the town behind him, these were few and far between. The velvet darkness of the countryside closed in on all sides. He closed his eyes tightly and then opened them slowly just as Uncle Barney had often told him to do but It made no difference.

There was no escaping the fact that the beginning of his journey had meant passing close to Bankside School. How strange it had looked by night! Empty and sad! Daniel had paused for a moment to cast a lingering look in the direction of the rows of blank windows before crossing the road to reach the railway bridge on the station side. There had been a little more light there and the possibility of reading the time on the station clock. Ten fifty-five. The pavements had been more or less deserted. Even the street children had finally made their way home to whatever sort of welcome awaited them; few cars had been about as cars cost money and petrol was in short supply. It had struck Daniel that, despite that, someone had disliked Ina and Billy enough to throw petrol at their caravan and set it alight! It kept running in his brain as he walked along. It made no sense, no sense at all!

Daniel had been more afraid of the dark than he would ever have been willing to admit but now it was his friend. As long as he could avoid drawing anyone's attention, he was safe. The night was his friend.

It was a long climb beyond the bridge, with the road disappearing over the brow of the hill. Next, the road dipped a little before turning to the left in a wide arc past several grand houses. One Saturday morning last winter, Uncle Barney had taken him along when he'd had to deliver coal to one of these. Daniel had marvelled that anyone could live in something so enormous and had been a little disappointed to discover that many of the largest houses had been turned into flats, housing not one family but several. A peep inside, however, had told him that these flats were far removed from those that were to be found in Abercrombie Terrace. They were huge! In addition, they had gardens, thickly wooded. In the leafy gateway of one of these gardens, Daniel stopped to rest. He could smell pine needles underfoot and hear the faint sound of music in an upstairs room. Someone was playing a piano and the sound drifted through an open window and across the garden. A girl was singing. She sounded happy.

Beyond this row of houses, Daniel kept close to the walls and hedges that bordered the pavement. He had to make sure that he would be able to see anyone approaching. He'd worn his sandshoes because they were best for climbing and now he was glad of that; they made virtually no sound as he picked his way through the darkness. Ahead of him, far off to his right, he could see a light that grew brighter and more interesting with every step he took. Better even than the welcoming light was the enticing smell. He was in luck! It was a chippie and it was open!

Unlike the grand houses further along the road, the shop was anything but smart. The floor was covered in sheets of old cardboard, presumably to soak up the grease from the fryers, while the customers - and there were several of these even at this late hour - had probably come from the nearby council estate, which clung to the side of the hill. On the wall behind the counter, a large notice reminded everyone not to ask for credit as it was against the house rules to give any! In heavy black type its message was clear: "Do not ask for credit as a refusal often offends". He wouldn't need credit. He had money!

Clutching his supper, Daniel melted back into the night as soon as he could. Pausing only to check that he was not being followed, he headed for the brow of the hill. No-one was following. He could slow down and enjoy his chips. How good they tasted! He'd asked for salt and vinegar but now he wasn't sure if that had been a good idea. His thirst was back with a vengeance and he hadn't dared to spend more money on something to drink. He tried not to think about it and concentrated on eating his supper while keeping a wary eye out for any stranger on the horizon.

On reaching The Boulevard, Daniel congratulated himself. He'd managed to remember the way. However, the traffic surprised him; some cars were still about, even at this time of night, heading in or out of the city seven miles away. Tall, amber street lights lit four lanes of traffic, two into the city and two out! Such vehicles as were still about were travelling at speed. He would have to be careful. If he were to miss his footing crossing here, he would stand little chance. No driver would see him until it was too late.

Without warning, it was there – right in front of him! The engine! He could see the man jump down on to the line. He could see the train, hear the roar of its breath. He could see the tiny boy, hear his cries and the sound of a woman screaming. It was a picture that came to him in sleep. He shook his head and the picture faded. It had all been a very long time ago. He'd been too small to remember and that was best. The metal plaque in Bankside Park with its own Memorial Garden, told the story for all to see. The date was there as was his father's name, Walter Abercrombie; below that was the name of the child, Robert Fairley, aged two years, also lost under the wheels of the train. It had all been for nothing. No-one talked about it very much when Daniel was around except to say that his father had been a brave man. Railway Terrace had been given a new name in his father's honour. Now and forever Daniel would be Daniel Abercrombie of Abercrombie Terrace, the son of Walter Abercrombie, a very brave man, a man he could barely remember, a man he'd never had the chance to know.

The wide carriageways, northbound and southbound, were separated by a broad expanse of grass. That was helpful. The lamps created occasional patches of extremely bright light, with dense darker areas in between. For reasons of safety, his own safety, Daniel chose a brightly lit patch. At the first gap in the traffic, he made for the middle of the highway. Once there, he threw himself flat and waited in the grass until his heart had stopped racing and the sound of disappearing traffic had faded. There was a sudden lull in the flow of southbound traffic so, with one final push, he was able to scramble across the carriageway and reach the safety of the far side.

Leaving the sound of traffic behind him, Daniel turned towards the village of Meldrum and the unlit road that lay between him and Glenderrin. This was "countryside dark" and it was different. Even though he opened and closed his eyes five times, it was still impossible to see more than a yard or two in front of him. Rooting in his rucksack, Daniel felt for his torch. There was nothing else for it. He would have to risk a light.

Meldrum was a small village on the way to nowhere, except, of course, Glenderrin. In the light of day, in all its glory, it could be seen for what it was - a place that time had somehow forgotten and passed by. The people of Meldrum liked it that way. They were more than grateful for the fact that the bombing that had ravaged the nearby towns had spared them from most of the horrors of the war, although the well-tended memorial cross in the centre of the village reminded all who passed that way that family members from this small community had lost their lives in two world wars. A wreath of scarlet poppies bore witness to the fact that they were not forgotten.

Meldrum was sleeping. Few cottages carried a light and the uneven, narrow lanes between the huddled houses made progress slow and hazardous. Several times, Daniel nearly lost his footing on the uneven ground while struggling to keep a firm grip on the torch. Here, in the dark, Meldrum had become a strange and fearful place where the risk of discovery was all too obvious. Here, a strange boy wandering about at this time of night would be out of the ordinary. If he were discovered, that would be the end of reaching Glenderrin and the end of finding Billy and Ina. There would be the local polis or the school's kid-catcher, who would make sure that Daniel was returned to the "appropriate authorities" and that would be the children's home - Percival House!

The sound of rushing water told him that he was approaching the mill somewhere up ahead on his left. Daniel now knew exactly where he was. He remembered that he'd been this way before - just once. Soon, any minute, the road should make a sharp turn to the left, which would put him on the winding lane that led to Glenderrin itself. It couldn't be far off now. Even in this gloom, the bend was easy enough to find. Once on the lane, he could simply keep to the hedgerow and feel his way. Easy! The darkness was thicker now but, strangely, that provided a sense of comfort. He could see only a few feet in front of him but that was the same for anyone else out there. All he had to do was keep his nerve and keep putting one foot in front of the other. The light from his torch might give him away but there were very few houses here, just the odd cottage or two and a row of smallholdings closer to Glenderrin itself. That much he did remember. Also, he remembered Uncle Barney telling him that country people went to bed early and rose with the morning sun. By morning, he hoped to be in Glenderrin. By morning, he hoped to have found Ina and Billy. There was no going back now!

Progress was slow and the occasional gateway or yard caused meanderings, which meant some retracing of his steps. Beginning to tire, Daniel stopped to get his bearings. He shone the torch around him. He wasn't sure but he imagined that somewhere to his right there had been the smallest of sounds as if someone or something was keeping him company. There it was again! A rustling in the leaves. Bigger than a hedgehog. Fox? Badger?

Low down and to his right, close to the boundary hedge, reflected in the beam of his torch, shone two bright eyes . He hadn't been mistaken. He wasn't alone and he was being watched. Keeping his back to the hedge, Daniel edged forward. The eyes kept him company. Bigger than a fox – and it was keeping him in its sights. The eyes, ever watchful, were following his every move. A soft whistle, somewhere up ahead, drew a quick response. The eyes disappeared. Daniel turned his head in the direction of the sound. A light was approaching. It was high in the air and making better progress than he was. Something brushed past him in the darkness. He felt its breath. Switching off his torch and taking refuge in the hedgerow, he waited.

"Is someone there?"

Daniel kept still and made no answer. It came again.

"Are you in trouble? Do you need help?" It was a woman's voice. It sounded kind.

Daniel switched on the torch once again and turned to face the approaching voice. "It's just me," he called out into the blackness beyond the feeble beam of light. He could just about make out the shape of a tall woman, carrying what looked like a large storm lantern. She was accompanied by a very large and very bouncy black and white collie dog, which kept closely to heel.

"Are you all right?" she asked. "I hope Max didn't frighten you. He isn't used to meeting wandering boys at this time of night and, for that matter, neither am I! Are you lost? It's very late."

"I'm not lost," Daniel replied. His voice sounded loud in the stillness. "I'm on my way to visit someone. I'm just a bit late in getting there but I do know my way. Your dog scared me. I couldn't really see him in the dark - just his eyes!"

The reply was immediate! "I'm sorry. We walk this lane most nights but we never meet a living soul so I think Max would be more afraid of you than you were of him. He's gentle and he likes people so don't worry about him. He won't hurt you. If you like, we can walk along together. I think you'll be able to see better by the light of my lantern than with that torch of yours."

The woman laughed and Daniel stopped being afraid but Uncle Barney had warned him about strangers. Strangers could be dangerous but this woman seemed kind and, in any event, he was sure he could outrun her if he had to, even in the dark. He wasn't quite so sure about the dog! Still, she was right about the lantern.

Keeping Max by her side, the woman turned back the way she'd come and Daniel fell in step beside her. The lantern lit the road ahead much better than Daniel's torch so they were able to keep up a steady pace.

"My name is Kitty," said the woman. "I live in Ivy House, which is just a few yards along this road. If you like, you can come in and rest for a while before going on. You look tired and, in any case, it's very late for you to be out and about especially on this lonely road. Are your friends expecting you? Will they be worried?"

Daniel thought for a moment before replying. "My friends don't know I'm on my way," he said. "It's going to be a surprise, you see!" He paused. "I'm not afraid of the dark. I used to be but I'm not now. I'm pretty good at looking after myself so I'm O.K. but I am thirsty. I'd be glad of a drink of water, if you don't mind. I suppose I didn't know how long it was going to take me, so I didn't bring a drink with me. I bought some chips, though. They were good."

Kitty laughed. "I thought I could smell vinegar," she whispered. "Now I understand!" Suddenly, they were there and Max ran on ahead of them.

Ivy House rose up out of the darkness on his right, its towering white gable end on to the road, its painted brickwork laced with the ivy that had given it its name; it clung even to the chimneys high above them. A small wooden gate opened inwards on to a gravel path that crunched beneath their feet as they made their way towards a sheltered doorway tucked away at the side of the building, a wooden porch protecting it from the weather. Through a tiny window to the right of the doorway, Daniel could see into a large kitchen, which was at the rear of the house. An oil lamp on the windowsill had been left burning and it lit the way.

Once inside, Kitty turned and closed the door, locking it behind them and hanging the key on a hook on the wall. Daniel thought about what Uncle Barney had said about not putting too much trust in strangers. Strangers could mean danger. However, If he had to, he was fairly sure he could reach that key.

Chapter 6

Ivy House and Beyond

Kitty crossed the room, with Max at her heels, and the old dog settled down in front of the fire, which was fading in the hearth. Kitty added a fresh log, levering it into position with a long brass poker. The firelight dimmed for a moment and then flickered into life. Daniel hesitated by the doorway and looked around him. The room was warm and almost impossibly tidy, with a place for everything and everything in its place. The kitchen looked so neat that it was hard to believe that anyone actually lived there. Close to the fire, was a large leather armchair with a bookcase, crammed with books, just beside it. The books were neatly ordered just like the rest of the room, the walls of which were lined with pictures and plates as well as old photographs. In the flickering light from the fire, it was impossible to make them out with any clarity. In the centre of the long oak table at one end of the kitchen was a vase of faded flowers. Kitty said nothing about it but removed it and placed it on the floor close to the door. The table was already set for two.

"I usually have some supper before I settle down for the night," said Kitty. "Would you like to join me? It would be nice to have some company for a change and you look as if you could do with something to warm you up." On the table, Daniel could see what looked and smelled like homemade bread and, beside that, a pot of jam. "It's strawberry," said Kitty, following his gaze, "Homemade!" Daniel didn't need to be asked twice.

Kitty made a pot of tea and they sat facing each other at the kitchen table just as if they were old friends, just as if this was something they had done many times before. Kitty spread some butter and jam on the crusty bread and pushed the plate towards Daniel. Hungry, despite the chips, Daniel didn't hesitate. Kitty ate her own supper and said very little. From time to time, however, Daniel looked up to find her watching him. She seemed to be waiting. Finally, while Kitty listened, he began to tell his story. By the light of the fire, he told Kitty about Uncle Barney and needing to find Billy and Ina. Now and again she would ask a question as if to make sure that she was following but, for most of the time, she listened without saying a word. She didn't look at the clock on the mantelpiece, nor did she show, even once, that she was tired. Once, she rose to put another log on the fire but, apart from that, Kitty left the table only to bring a hot drink for Daniel.

When he'd finished his supper and his tale, Kitty sat very still and quiet for a moment before saying anything." I should think there's every chance that your friend, O'Neill, is right and that Ina and Billy will be with Colonel McPhee," she said. "He's a good man and, if I'm right, he will do all that he can to help them and, perhaps, your Uncle Barney too. The colonel has two cottages close to the big house. He's been trying to rent them out for some time. One of them belongs to his daughter, Marianne, but she lives in London most of the year. Hers is a beautiful cottage but it's been empty for a while so he'd probably be glad to have someone living there again. Marianne loves the city but I've always believed her to be a country girl at heart. Some day she'll come back."

The warmth of the fire and the comfort of the supper began to have an effect. Daniel's eyelids felt heavy and his eyes longed to close in sleep. Over by the window, close to the fire, he noticed a couch. It had a pile of cushions at one end and a patchwork blanket neatly folded at the other. Kitty turned her head to follow his gaze. "That sofa was my own dear husband's favourite spot," she confided. "His name was Maurice and he died many years ago but, when he was a young man, he was a gypsy, a proper Romany with a horse and a caravan. He was so handsome! I ran away from home to marry him and we travelled far and wide together before we finally came back here to live in Ivy House. My family were angry with us at first but they came round in the end. Everyone loved Maurice, you see! He could charm the birds from the trees! I made that blanket while we were on the road. It gave me something to do in the long winter evenings. It's still as good as the day it was finished. Why don't you rest for a while, perhaps until the morning? Better than wandering the lanes at night. You can make an early start tomorrow. I don't expect your friends would be very happy to think of you out there in the night. By morning you might even be able to see where you're going!"

Daniel needed no persuading but, as he turned to leave the table, he froze. He was suddenly aware that he was being watched. From the depths of the armchair by the fire, a black cat was following his every move. Daniel was certain that the armchair had not been occupied when first he'd first entered the room.

"Don't worry about Mindy," said Kitty, "Max is a happy sort of chap but Mindy takes a bit of getting used to. She's old and more or less tolerates people so you'll be fine. It's other animals that have to be on their guard. Years ago, I put a sign on the gate. It's still there. It says - 'Beware Of The Cat!'"

As Kitty dimmed the lamp and placed a wire guard in front of the fire, Daniel settled himself on the couch and covered himself up with the blanket. It felt good. As she closed the kitchen door behind her, Kitty wished him a peaceful night but, before he could reply, she was gone. Max, with his head on his paws, closed his eyes and stretched out on the hearthrug. Mindy curled herself into a circle and fell asleep. Outside, in the woods beyond the garden, a solitary barn owl screeched and then fell silent. Unseen, in the orchard behind the cottage, a solitary fox picked his way between the plum trees and, high above the chimneys of Ivy House, the clouds parted to reveal a silver moon. By the roadside, the garden gate creaked on its hinges; a wooden sign held in place by one rusty nail carried the warning: "BEWARE OF THE CAT!"

Daniel heard the owl calling in the wood and drew the blanket more snugly up to his chin. Uncle Barney could make owl calls. He was good at it. He could even fool owls into thinking that a rival was on their patch! Daniel thought about that as he went to sleep, thought about Uncle Barney, wondered where he was sleeping and whether he was thinking about him. Tomorrow he would find Ina and Billy. Tomorrow he would get help for Uncle Barney – somehow!

He had no idea how long he'd slept but was awakened by the sound of Kitty busying herself in the kitchen. She was wrapped in a dusty coat and hat and looked as if she was ready to go out.

"Sorry to wake you, Daniel," she said, realising that he'd opened his eyes, "I'm just getting ready to start work on the garden. I like to get out there as soon as the sun is up. I like to work while everyone else is still in bed! It's a bit of a jungle out there. Without Maurice, I find it's a constant job so I have to keep at it!" Daniel was puzzled. He was standing by the front window and had a good view of the cottage garden and the lane beyond.

"But, everything looks perfect," protested Daniel. "You have a lovely garden."

"You're very kind," replied Kitty, "but I'm afraid that the back of this garden is not like the front. My dear grandson has been working hard on the rockery at the front but there's even more land at the back. My husband, Maurice, used to help me with the pond, the orchard and the woodland but, without him, it's got out of hand. He had a vegetable plot too and grew everything we needed. I liked that. Having our own home-grown things was a great help during the war. We kept several families going! Maurice also grew Christmas trees for the market. He loved it when everyone came to choose their trees just before Christmas and he would cut them down or dig them up, whatever they wanted, and I would make mince pies for all our customers and everyone would have a mince pie and a glass of ginger wine before they went off home again. It was the best part of getting ready for Christmas!"

A shadow seemed to pass over Kitty's face but she was soon smiling again. Buttoning up her coat, she collected a basket of gardening tools that stood waiting by the back door and called to Max and Mindy to follow her.

"I've left you some sandwiches on the kitchen table, Daniel," Kitty said, as she turned away. "You'll need something to eat as you head off. Oh, and there's a washroom in the extension at the back, if you want to tidy up before you go. You'll want to look smart for your friends."

"Thank you, Kitty. Thanks for helping me and everything," called Daniel after her disappearing figure. She paused on the back step and turned around.

"Happy to help! It was good to have your company. You can come back any time and bring your friends and your Uncle Barney next time. There will always be a warm welcome at Ivy House. Come as often as you like."

"If you like, we could maybe help you with the back garden," called Daniel."

"That sounds like a very good idea," replied Kitty. "We get deer and badgers and all sorts of visitors when the place is quiet so I think you might enjoy it here. Yes, come again. We'll consider that settled - a deal between us – and, in case I forgot to mention it, we still have some very fine Christmas trees looking for a home!" With a final wave of her hand and with Max and Mindy at her heels, she was, quite suddenly, gone.

It was time to move on. Daniel took a few minutes to have a wash and also to take one good look at the many pictures that lined the walls of the kitchen. Several were watercolours, signed with the initials, K. F. They were good. Here and there were photographs, family groups, faded prints of times gone by, smiling faces turned towards the camera. In one, propped up in pride of place on the mantel, he thought he recognised Kitty, herself; a smiling woman, younger then, her arms wrapped around two small boys, one taller than the other. They were laughing. When he turned it round to look at the back, someone had written: "Granny and her Boys".

Before letting himself out, Daniel took time to collect his sandwiches and took one last look around the empty room. Everything was just as neat as before, but he couldn't help noticing that the vase of faded flowers had been returned to pride of place in the middle of the kitchen table.

As he left, Daniel glanced to his right towards the back garden. He had a clear view of the land behind the cottage and now he could see exactly what Kitty had meant. All he could see was a tangle of overgrown bushes, long grass and thick undergrowth. A dirt path appeared to lead towards a wood that was almost out of sight at the far end of the garden. Daniel took a few steps along it to see if he could see Kitty but there was no-one there nor was there any sign of Max and Mindy, although, somewhere in the distance, a dog barked just once and then fell silent. A sudden flurry of chattering sparrows burst from the trees. Something had scared them. Then the garden settled and was still once more. Daniel took one last look before leaving. By the fence stood a row of Christmas trees of varying sizes and an untidy pile of logs that had tumbled on to the path. Just as he turned back towards the lane, Daniel thought he caught sight of a pair of sharp green eyes peering out between the branches of the last tree in the line. "Mindy?" he whispered but there was nothing there.

As he left, Daniel stopped to fasten the wooden gate. A frayed piece of old rope hung loosely from one gatepost and so he was able to make use of that but there was nothing he could do about the warning sign that swung precariously from one nail. "BEWARE OF THE CAT!"

Back in the lane, he began to hurry. However, after only a few steps, he stopped. Directly ahead of him, on the slow curve of the very next bend, stood two huge ornamental stone gateposts. The carved inscription on the right hand post clearly read, "Glenderrin House". The colonel was Kitty's neighbour. Ivy House was practically next door to the gates of the colonel's estate. Daniel looked back towards Ivy House. How strange that Kitty hadn't told him how close he had been to his journey's end! Still, the main thing was that he was here now.

In broad daylight, Daniel remembered having passed this way before with his Uncle Barney. There had been iron gates here at one time but they were gone now like all the other gates for miles around. He remembered Uncle Barney telling him about it. He'd said it was just the same as what had happened to the railings on The Crescent steps. Still, the park had kept its gates and fences. Probably, Duffy had defended those! Daniel smiled to himself as he imagined Duffy fighting off all-comers as they tried to remove his precious gates! No chance!

The stone gateway towered over him in all its splendour, its broad twin columns decorated with gargoyles, their grinning faces peering down at him. "The Girnin' Gates" Uncle Barney had called them. Now Daniel remembered why!

The driveway, rough and stony, disappeared from sight behind clumps of giant rhododendrons. Daniel kept to the grass at the side of the drive as it made for easier walking. It would also be easier for him to take cover if he suddenly had to disappear. He didn't want anything or anyone to stop him now. From what Kitty had said about the colonel, he was more sure than ever that he would be someone he could trust but he also remembered what The Devil had said about the shotgun. Best not to take any chances!

He tried not to think too much about what might be happening to Uncle Barney. He was probably in a jail cell. Daniel tried hard not to picture what that might be like. His uncle, Barney Abercrombie, was a good man. He was sure of that. But something was wrong, a "something" that followed him wherever he went, a new "something" that had arrived in recent weeks and hung over him like a dark cloud. Sometimes, it seemed as if Uncle Barney wanted to talk about it but the words seemed to get stuck and the moment would pass. Whatever it was, Daniel wished it would go away. Fortunately, he was close to thick undergrowth when the sound of a vehicle approaching down the stony driveway sent him diving for cover among the rhododendrons. Through the shiny leaves and mass of branches, he saw a car but it was unlike any car that he'd ever seen before. It was enormous! The coachwork gleamed shiny black in the morning sunlight and the engine made hardly a sound as it crunched the length of the rough gravel driveway. The driver wore a military-style cap and a dark green uniform; in the back seat Daniel thought he could see a single passenger but he wasn't certain. Soon the car was out of sight beyond the curve of the drive. Whoever lived here had lots of money. That was for sure!

Satisfied that the car was gone, Daniel emerged from his hiding place. He took time to remind himself what day it was. Saturday! Esther! She would be worrying, trying to work out where he could be and what he would be doing. What would she think if she could see him now? On Saturdays, he and Esther would go into Riverside and head for the library there. After they'd handed back their old books and chosen some new ones for the week, they would head for Woolworth's to buy sugarolly, then go on to the paper shop for comics. Instead of catching the tram, they'd walk home along the main road, so they could save their fares for buying penny caramels and home-made ice lollies at Jenny's Café through the week after school. That's what he should be doing now - heading for the library with Esther. Still, being here was better than being in Percival House with the Welfare breathing down his neck! That thought cheered him on.

As he picked his way over the uneven ground, Daniel looked around him. The estate was a mixture of rough grassland and patches of wilderness; it had a neglected air about it and yet had a grandeur all of its own. The trees that edged the drive stretched high above Daniel's head, their overhanging branches blocking out most of the sunlight so that it was cool beneath the leafy canopy. Then, all at once, he was back out in the sunlight as the grounds opened up and the trees were replaced by a tidy hedge of clipped privet and yew. The drive became smoother and Daniel guessed that he must be getting nearer to Glenderrin House, itself. The next turn, however, led him not to a fine house but to a low block of crumbling buildings, which looked as if they had once been farm workers' cottages. The barred windows and half-doors suggested that they were now being used as stables. From somewhere up ahead came the clattering of metal buckets and the sound of grumbling voices. Daniel stopped. It crossed his mind that here he might be able to ask for help but the cursing and the anger in the voices made him think again. He kept perfectly still and pressed himself against the red brick wall of the gable, out of sight. Then, taking care to make no sound, he crept nearer to an open door at the middle of the building. He was pretty sure that he could hear without being seen. However, he would have to keep his wits about him and be ready to run if anyone appeared in that doorway.

There were two voices, rough and angry – two men calling to each other as they worked. It sounded as if they were clearing out old straw bedding and making heavy weather of it. The scraping of their shovels on the stone floor was a familiar sound, often heard in the coal yard where Uncle Barney worked. Most of the cursing that he could hear was directed towards "Old McPhee".

From where he was standing, Daniel couldn't see either of the two men but he was able to work out that one of them, the louder and more roughly spoken of the two, was called Birdie, while the other was Midge. Birdie appeared to be in charge of things while Midge sounded scared as well as angry. Whatever Birdie said, Midge agreed with! It seemed that, in the absence of Colonel McPhee, their employer, the two men were taking the opportunity to call him every name under the sun.

Suddenly, to Daniel's alarm, he realised that they were about to down tools. The shovels were noisily thrown down on to the stone floor, which sent Daniel scurrying past the open door and round to the far end of the building. Just as quick as going back! Crouching down behind some straw bales, he was out of sight and ready to run, if he had to. Clutching his rucksack, Daniel held his breath. He didn't have long to wait.

Chapter 7

The Golden Boy

"Same as always!" It was Birdie who was first to speak. "We clean up after those wretched animals of his, while he goes swanning off to Edinburgh. His Lordship says it's business – but we know better! McPhee will be stuffing his face at that club of his, boring everybody with his life story, telling them all about his army days and hanging about with his old cronies while Mitchell struts around in that monkey suit of his!"

Midge was quick to agree. "In other words, the usual Saturday! Mitchell dressed up like a dog's dinner while we do all the dirty work and get paid peanuts for our trouble!" This was followed by a great deal of cursing and the sound of a bucket being kicked across the cobbled yard.

It was Birdie, the larger of the two men, who spoke

next. He sounded pleased with himself about something. "Well, this time it's going to be different. His Lordship is in for a surprise when he gets back!" Another bucket went flying across the yard, clattering against the wall of a stone outhouse.

"Will we have time?" Midge sounded anxious.

"Oh yes, we'll have plenty of time. I heard our dearly beloved colonel telling Mitchell that he's staying in town tonight at his club. When he does that our dear Mitchell makes the most of it. He'll spend his free time in the town at the dog track and, when he isn't there, he'll be strutting his stuff in that fancy gear of his and looking around to see who's looking at him! He was talking to himself in the hall mirror just before they left. Daft as a brush, if you ask me! When he saw I was watching, he just laughed – gave me a salute – and laughed!"

"No wonder he was so cheerful," growled Midge. "He's the one smelling of roses while we do the mucking-out! He's having an easy time while we slave away! In his shoes, I'd be laughing!"

Daniel could smell cigarette smoke. He knew that was a bad sign. Mr Gilligan and Uncle Barney would never allow matches and cigarettes anywhere near the coal yard stables. Matches and dry straw – a bad combination!

Daniel flattened himself against the wall as Birdie's voice rang out once again, loud and clear. "Don't you worry, we'll have the last laugh when all this is done and we've got our own place down under! Australia, here we come! Today's the day, Midge! Nobody about! Today's the day we put some real money in our pockets. Don't you forget that! Our turn's coming!"

Daniel could hear the men laughing. It sent chills down his spine. If he could have made a dash for it, he would have. If he could have stopped listening, he would have. No! There could be no running, not without giving himself away, and so there could be no escape from what was to follow. All he could do was listen.

Midge was the first to speak, his voice quieter now and anxious. "When's the truck due?"

"Riley will collect him this afternoon and leave the money, as agreed, while we're at The Cross," answered Birdie. He spoke with smug satisfaction. "We'll make sure everybody sees us. A few drinks and a laugh in The Woodman after we've picked up the feed, followed by a nice stroll round the market, maybe a bit of a loud argument with Turnip Thompson on the veg. stall. That should do the trick! By the time we get back, the golden boy will be gone and we'll have our money for Australia, end of story!"

"What about the money?" asked Midge. "Are you sure it's going to be enough?" He sounded nervous.

'Don't you worry about the money. That's all sorted." Birdie crossed the yard to collect the bucket and, for a brief moment, Daniel was able to catch a glimpse of him. Birdie was a big man, a very big man, and heavily built. He was dressed in faded blue overalls that had seen better days. A filthy cloth cap was pushed to the back of his head. He didn't walk. He swaggered.

The other man, Midge, was much smaller in stature and was wearing a dusty suit that looked as if it had once belonged to someone much larger. When he spoke, his voice shook.

"Birdie, just remember - I'm your partner in all this - and that means I have a right to know what's going on. There's something you're not telling me, something about the money! Come on. I know when you're up to something. I want the truth!"

There was a pause that suggested Birdie was deciding whether or not to answer. "Well?" Midge was not about to be put off!

"How does a thousand sound to you?" There was a short pause. When the smaller man spoke, there was no mistaking the fear in his voice. "We don't need as much as a thousand, Birdie. You said three hundred for the horse would do the trick." The reply was immediate and brooked no contradiction!

"O.K. The fares are cheap for now but, if we're going to make it big in Australia, we'll need cash to set ourselves up when we get there. I'm not going to make the same mistakes I made here. If you don't want in then that's up to you but, with some real money, we can have our own place, not work for some other slave-driver like McPhee!" There was a pause before Birdie continued. "McPhee keeps a nice round thousand in the safe in his study. He was talking about it to that daughter of his a week or two back when she was here. I just happened to be weeding the beds right outside the open window. Couldn't help overhearing, if you know what I mean!"

Midge gave a low whistle. "I'm in, Birdie. We're in this together. You know that - but are you sure about this? A thousand's a lot of money. If this goes wrong..." His voice tailed off. "Anyway, if all this money is nice and tidy in the colonel's safe, how do we get at it? We'd need help with that kind of stuff. Riley might know someone."

"Aha!" Birdie was triumphant! "Apart from his beloved daughter, who visits him once in a blue moon, what is the most important thing in old McPhee's life?" Before Midge could reply, he answered his own question. "Boy Wonder, in there! Stuck on the wall in that study is a painting of the horse and behind that is the safe. McPhee was explaining it all to the darling daughter so I thought I might as well listen in! Thought it might come in handy. Want to make a guess at the combination? Any numbers come to mind?"

Midge mumbled something that Daniel couldn't quite hear but Birdie ignored him. "What's the height of that horse in there?" There was silence while Midge considered his reply.

"I reckon he's about eighteen hands. That right?"

"Close enough. He's seventeen and a half,17.2, and that's the code for the safe! 172172! Easy as pie! I heard McPhee reeling it off to the daughter so she could write it down in her diary or something. Clear as day! You don't have to be a master criminal to be one step ahead of those two."

Daniel heard the sound of a match being struck as someone lit up for a second time. There was the sound of the heavy, wooden door being pulled shut followed by the ringing of a long bolt into its place.

"It's a bit risky, Birdie. Let's just stick to what we'd agreed with Riley. We take the three hundred from Riley, the money for the horse, and make the best of it. Our bags are packed and the boat sails next week. Nobody knows we're going and there's nothing to tie us up with any of it. We'll be on the other side of the world in a few weeks. It's simple! Riley gets the horse and we get the money. Let's keep it that way. Let's just keep it simple! The colonel won't be sorry to see us go; he's threatened us with the sack often enough! Friend Mitchell will just have to do a bit more work around here until some other mugs turn up! Please, Birdie. I'm not sure about this!" His whining voice was pleading but his words were falling on deaf ears. Birdie was not about to give way.

"Look! We just report the theft of the horse. We're in the clear. Security round here is a joke. Not our fault if McPhee's too mean to spend money on decent locks. As for the horse, Riley will make sure he's well drugged up and rugged up but his mate on the Irish boat won't be asking too many awkward questions anyway. He owes Riley a few favours so there won't be any problems. Once the boat docks on the other side, the horse and Riley disappear. Riley will get a few foals from him and make himself plenty of cash for his own plans. We don't need to know anything about that. So far, that golden wonder has passed on his colour to all his foals and that's worth real money to Riley! As a bonus, we can watch McPhee suffer before we go! I'm looking forward to that nearly as much as the money! Ireland's a good place to lose a horse but if it does start to attract the wrong kind of attention, it disappears for good, if you get my meaning!"

"How do you mean? Midge continued to sound uneasy.

"Dog meat!" came the immediate reply.

In response to more questions from his anxious partner, Birdie was working hard to calm him down. "Three hundred from Riley and a thousand from the colonel's safe. It's all worked out. Enough to pay for our tickets and plenty to spare. That's proper money. We can set ourselves up with our own place and no mistake! We have the perfect opportunity right now so let's get on with it and stop wasting time!"

Midge sounded more afraid than ever. "The safe? Right now? We'll be in the frame straight off," he cried. "We're the only ones around."

"McPhee won't realise the money's gone – not for days. We'll leave everything neat and tidy. He'll be too busy looking for his precious horse and no-one'll be able to prove anything against us. Anyway, my guess is the old goat won't be in a position to make a fuss about it, because he's probably hiding the money from the tax man. There's nothing to worry about. No problem! I'll do the safe. I'll wear gloves. That's what they do in the films. I happen to know that the study window is off the latch. I made sure of that when I took the papers in this morning so it'll be plain sailing and, by this afternoon, the horse will be gone and we'll be rich! What about it? Are you in or not?"

Midge didn't hesitate for long. "OK, Birdie, I'm in," he mumbled, "but I want to be kept in the picture. I'm not going to be kept in the dark on this. Where exactly is Riley leaving our money – the three hundred for the horse? You haven't even told me that. What's happening?"

There was a short pause before Birdie made his reply. "OK. The coast is clear for this afternoon. McPhee's old housekeeper's off visiting her sister, staying over until tomorrow, so we can take our time, do what we need to do and then we'll head for the market. This place will be as quiet as the grave. Riley'll pick up the horse about two when we're safely away from here and in the clear. He'll leave the three hundred, as agreed. I'll show you where. Don't you worry about that! But - Riley knows nothing about the safe and we need to keep it that way. That's between you and me and you'd better remember that!" There was menace in his voice.

Midge got the message! "You know me, Birdie. You can trust me."

Daniel tried to hear what was coming next! When Birdie spoke again, it was clear that he was thinking aloud and also making sure that his partner would know exactly what was expected of him. "We'll take the handcart for the feed. That makes plenty of noise so that's to the good. We make sure everyone sees us at the market. When we get back, we discover the horse is missing and report it. The telephone at the big house is out of order so by the time we stroll up to the lodge and get Mitchell's missus to phone the polis, the Irish boat'll be well on its way to the Emerald Isle. Riley will have the horse and we'll have our money for Australia and everybody's happy."

"Except the colonel," added Midge.

"Except the colonel!" The two men laughed.

"But what do we do with the thousand? We can't just keep it in our back pockets. It's too risky, Birdie. What do we do with it until next week?"

Birdie was not to be distracted. "Leave the thinking to me. It's in the bag! Now, let's get on with it!"

Daniel listened as the sound of heavy footsteps faded into the distance, presumably heading for Glenderrin House. For some reason, he must have missed the turning leading to the big house; he supposed it must have been hidden by the trees. From his hiding place, he could see very little but one thing was clear: he'd heard more than enough to put himself at risk. If Birdie and Midge had even an inkling that their plans had been overheard, there was no knowing what they might be prepared to do. Birdie, in particular, sounded as if he would stop at nothing.

Finally, all was quiet. Checking that he was indeed alone, Daniel stepped out into the yard. It was deserted. To his left was the stable door and he could see straight away that it was firmly bolted. With trembling fingers, he eased back the long, metal bolt and the huge door swung towards him, its weight providing momentum. Familiar smells drew him further in and he was reminded at once of many weekends spent helping Uncle Barney at Mr Gilligan's. This, however, was not the coal yard; this was something very different. Directly in front of him was a loose box, which, at first glance, appeared to be empty. However, the rustling of a hay net suggested otherwise. Daniel stood still and waited. He was not to be disappointed.

The horse leaned out towards him over the lower half of the stable door then, lifting its head high above him, it fixed him with a steady gaze. Even in this dim light, Daniel could see its smooth coat, a coat that shone like golden silk. Its mane was long and flowing and pale cream in colour. An embroidered head collar of fine tan leather bore a name, picked out in golden letters: "Midas".

Daniel reached out a nervous hand to stroke the velvet nose. Despite its size – and the horse was enormous – it had a kind eye and was happy to let him move closer so that he could reach up to stroke its neck. It nodded as if to encourage him and, as it did so, its silken mane brushed against Daniel's outstretched fingers. No wonder the colonel was a proud man!

To his left, through a wide doorway, Daniel could see a long stable block divided into seven individual stalls, all of which were empty. It was clear from the damp floor that this part of the building had recently been washed and brushed, presumably by Birdie and Midge before they'd downed tools. Pools of soapy water lay here and there on the stone floor, drying in the morning sun as it filtered through the tiny windows high above him. The air was sweet with the scent of fresh hay, disinfectant and saddle soap. Comforting smells!

Softly, Daniel closed the huge door behind him, taking care not to rattle the bolt, and made his way into the stable itself, stepping clear of the soapy puddles so that no footprints would show he'd ever been there. He would just take a quick look around and then he would have to think. There must be something he could do! He wished Uncle Barney were there. He would know what to do. Perhaps if he pretended that Uncle Barney were there, an idea would take shape. It was up to him now to rescue this horse, but how was he to do that?

Daniel tried to think what his uncle might say. If Uncle Barney could see him now, he would probably tell him to get out of there and find Ina and Billy, who would know exactly what to do. Not much one boy could do on his own! That made sense. He would stick to his original plan, find Ina and Billy as fast as possible and tell them everything. He would be safe and so would the horse but would there be time? What if he couldn't find Billy and Ina? What then?

Loud voices just outside the door interrupted his thoughts. Birdie and Midge! They were back! Daniel took cover where he could.

"I thought you shot this bolt, Midge?"

"I did. You saw me do it. You were there so don't start on me. I know for sure that this door was bolted when we left!" Daniel heard the door being pushed wider, This was followed by the ominous sound of heavy footsteps.

Holding his breath and clutching his rucksack tightly in both hands Daniel curled himself into a tight ball underneath a pile of straw that lay in the very last stall in the line. The straw was clean and sweet but it scratched his skin and tickled his nose. He shut his eyes tightly, held his breath and prayed that he wouldn't sneeze.

"Somebody's been here!" Midge sounded scared.

"Gypsies!" responded Birdie. "I'd put money on it!"

"They're up on Green Lane," offered Midge "Been there for days and they look like they're settling themselves in as usual."

Birdie growled! "There's always trouble when they're here. Still, they've made a run for it; must've heard us coming."

As if to make sure that he was right, Birdie marched the full length of the block. Daniel heard the scrape of his boots as he checked every stall, pausing at the last, where Daniel lay. He gave the piled up straw a cursory poke with a pitchfork that just happened to be resting against the wall. It missed Daniel by a whisker! Reassured that any intruder had cleared off, the boots and their owner made their way back to the main door. How could Daniel have failed to hear those terrifying feet coming towards him when there had been time to run?

"Now that I think of it, those gypsy lads could come in handy for once," announced Birdie. "The polis'll waste a few hours searching for McPhee's horse in Green Lane, if we point them in that direction. Gypsies like horses, don't they? I seem to remember that a couple of them do odd jobs for old Fergie up on the hill. We'll just say we've seen them hanging around the yard and looking as if they were up to no good. It'll buy Riley even more time!" There was a muttered exchange between the two men, followed by the sound of a heavy object of some kind being dragged across the floor. When next he spoke, Birdie sounded pleased with himself.

"We can leave it there for now. Riley knows to leave the three hundred under here. That's all arranged. When we get back we'll put the whole lot together and take it to Mandalay. No-one will think to look there. Safe as in a bank, it'll be!"

"I hope you're right!" Midge's voice trembled as he spoke.

For a brief moment, all was quiet and then came a sound that made Daniel's heart sink. It was the unmistakable clatter of a metal bolt being driven into place. He was locked in!

Chapter 8

No Way Out

The footsteps faded and all was quiet once again. Dusting himself down, Daniel emerged from his hiding place, gingerly retraced his steps past the pools of spilled water and stopped at the solid wooden door, testing it to see if it would give. It didn't move an inch.

Midas had returned to the cool, dark depths of his box, leaving Daniel to his own devices. Daniel could hear him tugging at a hay-net. Beyond this stone-flagged area was an office, which was obviously used as a tack room. Documents lay in untidy piles on a large roll top desk to his left. Two small windows, high up close to the ceiling, looked as if they hadn't been opened in years and clearly offered no way of escape. However, at the far end of this room, tucked away in the corner, almost out of sight, was a black spiral staircase, which had to lead somewhere.

Slipping his rucksack over his shoulders, so that both hands were free, Daniel made for the stairs. The desk may have been untidy but the room itself was neat and well ordered. The fresh, clean smell of saddle soap was familiar, a reminder of helping Uncle Barney with the harness for the coal yard ponies but the gleaming leather that was displayed around these whitewashed walls was quite unlike the motley collection to be found at the coal yard. This was very different. Daniel ran his fingers over the straps of a bridle, which hung on a hook by the door. It was soft like window leather. The noseband was broad and wrapped in snow-white sheepskin.

What next caught his eye, however, was a large corn bin, with a metal lid. It stood by the door and, judging by the scratch marks on the floor, it had recently been moved. Daniel guessed that this could explain the scraping sounds that he'd heard earlier. Lifting the lid, he peered inside. Just corn!

Midas's head reappeared over the stable door; he knew what the rattle of this bin could mean. This was the second time he'd heard this familiar sound in the last half hour and he was not planning on being disappointed once again! Used to making his desires known, the golden horse rattled the lower stable door with his foot. Then, with his ears pricked, he fixed an eager eye on the corn bin and, tossing his silken mane, nodded his head in expectation. The rattling and banging grew louder and the door creaked on its hinges. His message couldn't have been plainer!

He had to put a stop to this noise. Reaching into the bin, Daniel scooped up a handful of corn and offered it to a grateful Midas. Some of the fine corn slipped between Daniel's shaking fingers, scattering across the floor. Reaching down deep into the corn once again, he produced a second handful and, thankfully, the banging stopped. However, as he replaced the lid, something caught his eye; partly buried in the corn was something blue. At first glance, it looked like a piece of paper but, on closer inspection, Daniel realised that it was the corner of a large, blue envelope. One good tug released it, spilling more grains of corn on the dusty floor. Now he could see exactly what it was. No ordinary envelope, it was more like a package and it was stuffed with something. Remembering what he'd heard, Daniel had a good idea what this blue package contained but he knew there was only one way to know for sure. The flap was sealed but it was easy enough to tear it open. Inside, there was more money than Daniel had ever seen in his life before! He hesitated for only a moment before packing it into his rucksack. He had no idea where he was going but, wherever he ended up, the colonel's money was going with him.

At the foot of the metal staircase was a notice board, which had been fixed to the tack room wall. Daniel couldn't help stopping to look at the photographs and press cuttings that were pinned up on it. A headline caught his eye: "THE GOLDEN BOY DOES IT AGAIN!" The report and pretty much everything else on the board featured horse shows, local and national, where Midas was obviously something of a star. Ridden by a dark-haired girl, perhaps Marianne, the colonel's daughter, the golden horse was jumping gates and fences as well as being presented with silver cups and red ribbons. The wall beside the notice board was decorated with rosettes. This horse was a winner! No wonder the colonel was proud of him. But, if Birdie and Midge had their way, this horse was about to disappear.

No more delay! Daniel knew he had to get out and the staircase looked like his only hope. It was an awkward climb with his precious rucksack trailing over his shoulder and the stone walls closing in on him as he climbed. Finally, on the very last step, he was able to take a good look around him. A vast loft stretched before him. It was just as long as the stables below. Clearly used for storage, it was, for the most part, empty, except for random piles of old cardboard boxes, buckets, plant pots, ancient harness, scruffy wellington boots and heaps of binder twine. Mostly, it looked like junk!

The wooden boards creaked as he crossed the floor. To his right, something, a mouse perhaps, scuttled for cover. Daniel paused, but only for a moment. There was no time to lose. He had to find something that would get him out of here but what? It was probably a forlorn hope. Nothing sprang to mind! A face by the skylight stopped him in his tracks. Dark, unseeing eyes fixed him with an empty stare. For a moment, he froze and then he knew it for what it was. This was a face he'd met before. He remembered the cloying, sickening smell of rubber and the feel of the rough canvas on his skin. Uncle Barney had kept his old gas mask at the back of his wardrobe and, for all Daniel knew, it was there still. He'd come across it one day when he was helping to sort out some old clothes for the Salvation Army. He'd never forgotten it. Sometimes, even now, he would see it in his dreams. More than once, Uncle Barney had come running to see why he'd cried out in the night. He'd tried explaining to Daniel that the mask had been there to keep him safe from poison gas during the war and that it was nothing to be afraid of but those dark, sightless eyes staring out from the depths of the wardrobe haunted him still.

This gas mask was hanging next to a small skylight. The cracked glass, green with moss, let some light into the dusty attic. It was one of a long line of matching windows, which struggled to brighten the bleak interior, sending dusty rays of warmth through the stale air.

Avoiding the tangled heaps of knotted twine and collections of assorted relics, Daniel made his way towards the second skylight. It was the cleanest in the line, less green than the others. It appeared to be partially open – but not by much! Enough, perhaps?

The rusty hinges of the crumbling window frame were stiff but, to his relief, he was able, with one mighty heave, to force it open, creating a way out on to the pantiles. The rush of fresh air felt good. Using an old metal bucket as a makeshift step, he was able to squeeze his head and shoulders through the gap. To his surprise, Daniel found that he could now see for a long, long way, peering through the straggly tops of the conifer hedge that marked the boundary between the stables and the world beyond. One more push and Daniel was able to wriggle through and climb up on to the sloping tiles of the roof itself. The bucket rattled as it rolled away and, unnerved by the sudden noise in the midst of silence, he almost lost his balance but, somehow, he managed to cling on to the window frame. It creaked and threatened to give way but, to his relief, it held fast, providing him with time to find a foothold on the mossy roof.

The roof was steep and, by the time he'd climbed up, using the edges of the red pantiles for purchase, he was, according to his own estimate, about twenty feet from the ground. Trees were one thing but this was quite another! Branches create a ladder but there was nothing here to suggest an easy way down. Two tall turrets rising through the trees to his right almost certainly belonged to Glenderrin House. Below, at the rear of the stable block, was a narrow pathway and then the conifer hedge. Daniel ruled that out as an escape route immediately. The front of the stable block faced the cobbled yard; that would also be a dangerous option. Remembering the pile of straw bales at the far end of the building, Daniel decided to head in their direction. The bales would break his fall and cushion his landing if he could manage to slither down the wall, or even jump for it! Worth a try!

Climbing on to the ridge tiles, he lay flat and began to pull himself towards the gable end of the stable block. The rucksack was a burden but he dared not let it go. He paused only once to ensure that the bag was securely fastened and its contents safely stowed inside. Yes - the blue envelope was still there, bulging with one thousand pounds of the colonel's money. Birdie was going to be looking for that sooner or later!

The sudden sound of a vehicle fast approaching down the moorland path made him freeze; he was in full view and there was nowhere to hide. He would have to hope that the driver would be too busy keeping an eye on the winding lane to look upwards. A quick glance was all he dared but it was enough to tell Daniel that the vehicle was a jeep and that it was being driven wildly and at speed.

Gears grinding, it sped past, towing a battered trailer in which he could see three, maybe four, black and white sheepdogs. It was difficult to be sure. The animals were struggling to keep their feet, the vehicle swaying violently as it negotiated the twists and turns of the narrow lane.

From the stable roof, Daniel watched as it made its winding way towards the main road, which he estimated was about three hundred yards away beyond a clump of trees. In moments, it was out of sight and Daniel breathed a sigh of relief.

Turning to look in the direction from which the jeep had approached, Daniel could see nothing but open grassland, moorland stretching as far as the eye could see. It was dotted with gorse bushes, rocky outcrops and the occasional clump of trees as well as sheep - hundreds and hundreds of sheep! The entrance to this wild and lonely place was marked by a broad cattle grid and, to its left, a five-barred gate. Beyond that point, the road became a rough, stony lane. Probably not much traffic came this way. There had to be a farmhouse over the brow of the hill and out of sight; the driver and his dogs had to live somewhere! Straddling the ridge tiles, the germ of an idea spurred him on and, by the time he'd reached the gable end, Daniel knew exactly what he needed to do. Before he could do anything, however, he had to get down. He would have to jump. The bales would provide an easier landing than the yard. He would have to take the chance. But – it was a long drop! He thought of his father. His father had jumped. Daniel had a clear picture of that in his mind. He carried it with him and probably always would. He hadn't been there when his father had jumped. He'd been very small but he knew the story only too well. In his worst nightmares, he often saw his father jump - jump down on to the line, pick up the boy – a boy about the same age as Daniel was at that time– and try to reach the safety of the platform. There would be the roar of the oncoming train and the voices shouting. Then, nothing. Just blackness - and the sound of the train – and the rushing of the steam and his mother crying. It was always the same.

Clinging to the edge of the roof, Daniel lowered himself until his arms were at full stretch. He closed his eyes and let himself go. It was more of a fall than a jump but the straw bales were enough to cushion the landing. He was down and, amazingly, apart from a small scratch on his right knee, he was unhurt.

Now what? He could run - make a dash for it down the lane towards the cottages he'd spotted from the roof. Perhaps Billy and Ina would be there – and he would be safe. No – too easy! He'd heard too much and he couldn't pretend he hadn't. There was something he had to do while there was still time! The sun was lower in the sky now, well past mid-day. There couldn't be much time left. Finding Ina and Billy would have to wait – at least for now!

Daniel turned back towards the stable door. With one firm pull, he slid the bolt free and dragged the heavy door back. Sunlight streamed into the warmth of the stable and an expectant golden head appeared at once. More corn, perhaps? On the desk by the door was a packet of biscuits and a few bruised apples in a brown paper bag. Daniel found room in his rucksack for these. He was hungry. It was stealing but he would put things right when he could. He had to go – but now he wouldn't be going alone!

Grateful for the tangled pile of binder-twine, Daniel helped himself to several strands and twisted them together to make a stronger cord. Distracting Midas with one of the apples, he threaded the cord through a ring on the horse's head collar and tugged at it gently to make sure that it would hold. It did!

Carefully slipping the bolt on the loose-box door, Daniel encouraged Midas to follow him out into the empty stable yard. The horse was even bigger than he had expected. Now it was plain to see! He was huge! Thankfully, however, he was gentle and eager to please. His head high in the air, he willingly followed Daniel into the yard. Almost as soon as he was outside, he began calling loudly to the ponies in the paddock. They were quick to respond!

"We're not going that way, urged Daniel, concerned that this was going to be more difficult than he had anticipated. If Birdie and Midge heard the animals' restless calls, they would be on top of him in a shot! "Come on, Midas, we're going this way!"

It took several firm tugs to turn the reluctant horse away from the paddock and back towards the moor but, in the end, with a final call to his friends in the field, he walked beside Daniel obediently enough. The rucksack was of great interest to him, perhaps because he could smell the apples! The main gate presented no problems as it had been left wide open, probably to make it easier for Riley and his truck! Turning towards the expanse of moorland, however, Daniel now faced the difficulty of holding on to the enormous horse while he struggled with the metal hook that secured the five-barred gate. Crossing by means of the cattle-grid was out of the question so the gate was his only option and it would have to be negotiated somehow! Vital time was being lost and, without a watch, Daniel could not be sure how much time he had left. By two o'clock, Riley and his van would be arriving and Riley would be expecting this horse to be waiting for him. Daniel couldn't even be sure that, by now, Birdie and Midge had left for town. He supposed they must have!

Most of the sheep were far away on the open moorland so at least Daniel didn't have to bother about them but it was as he led Midas through the gate and out on to the moor that he heard the sudden throb of an engine. A large vehicle was approaching down the lane. It sounded like a bus or a truck. It had to be Riley!

With his aching fingers tugging frantically at the tangled twine of his makeshift leading rein, Daniel led Midas out on to the moorland fell. The cord twisted around his fingers and so valuable moments were lost while he struggled to free himself. Then, all at once, the cord fell free and Midas was loose on the moor. He expected the animal to disappear over the hill in seconds but, to his horror, Midas just stood stock still and looked back at Daniel as if to say, "What now?"

The approaching vehicle was growing louder! "Go on!" shouted Daniel, "Run! Run!" He began waving his arms in desperation. The vehicle, whatever it was, sounded very close. Once it rounded the final bend in that lane he knew that he and the horse would be in full view. Midas trotted almost half-heartedly towards the open moor, his head low, close to the ground, as if savouring the scent of the sweet green grass, then, as if suddenly catching the breeze, he lifted his head high in the air and flew. He was free.

As Daniel watched, the golden horse disappeared over the brow of the hill. He was gone! Whatever else was out there on the moor, Daniel was quite sure that it was preferable to Riley and his van! Midas, at least, was safe - but was *he*? He wasn't quite so sure about that!

He'd planned to return to the stable before moving on. He didn't want to leave any clues for Birdie and Midge but there was no time for that now. As Daniel finally dared to turn and look back towards the gate, the truck came into full view. It was too far away to see the driver clearly so he couldn't be sure whether Riley had spotted him or not. It had to be Riley and he was about to find out that the horse he'd been promised was gone!

Fastening the moor gate seemed to take forever but he knew he had to do that in order to make sure that neither Midas nor the sheep wandered into danger by that route and Daniel's fingers shook as he struggled to secure the catch. The truck was slowing now as it approached the entrance to the yard. Time was running out. One final check on the catch and Daniel turned towards the moor. He had to put as much distance as possible between himself and Riley. Riley was not going to be a happy man!

Racing towards the shelter of a small copse, he realised that he would never get there in time. Throwing himself to the ground behind a clump of gorse, he kept his head down, shut his eyes and lay flat. Suddenly remembering that the bulging rucksack could give him away, he wriggled it from his shoulders and pulled it down beside him. It was heavy with the weight of the food he'd taken and, most importantly, the blue envelope. He tried not to think about how much money he was carrying.

Raising his head just a fraction, Daniel could see a plain, unmarked cattle truck. There was no lettering on the side to identify the driver but the large man in blue overalls climbing down from the driver's cab had to be Riley. He was looking all around as if to make certain that he was alone. Perhaps he hadn't seen Daniel after all! The man made no move towards the moor but climbed back up into his cab and drove slowly into the empty yard. It was an awkward entrance for such a large vehicle so it took a few minutes to negotiate. Finally, the engine fell silent which told Daniel that he had moments – only moments – before Riley would discover that the horse was gone.

Keeping a firm hold on his rucksack, Daniel began to run. The trees were about a hundred yards ahead of him and close to the brow of the hill. If he could reach them before Riley re-appeared, he might have a chance! It was rough going. If he fell, he would be caught for sure - but his luck held.

Once in the safety of the trees, he peered through the branches and back down the hill towards the stable buildings. Nothing moved. Everything was still. From the dark shelter of the trees, Daniel watched and waited. It wouldn't take too long for Riley to realise that his plans had come adrift. He'd come to collect a horse, a valuable horse. Now, someone had got in his way. Something had gone wrong. He wasn't going to like it. Daniel guessed, from what he'd overheard, that Riley had been told to leave the money for the horse underneath the corn bin. There would be no money now! No horse! No money! There would be three angry men, not one!

The copse was a mixture of evergreens and other trees. Hollies jostled for light with mountain ash and silver birch but, oddly, closer to the centre, a beech stood taller than the rest. Manoeuvring his rucksack firmly into place, Daniel gritted his teeth and began to climb. From high in its branches, he had a clear view of the entrance to the moor. His heart pounding, he watched as Riley came into view. He was a huge man, thick-set. Daniel watched as he scanned the horizon. Then, as he turned to go, Riley suddenly stopped and bent down to examine the soft earth by the cattle grid. Daniel had noticed some mud there and had tried to avoid it but, looking down now at his shoes, he realised that he must have left clear footprints. His footprints would run alongside those of the horse. He watched as Riley unhooked the gate and took a few steps out on to the open moor. His gaze swept across the wide expanse of grassland and then became fixed as he turned to look towards the copse. He took a few steps and then stopped in his tracks. He'd made his decision!

It must have taken only a few seconds for Riley to come to the conclusion that lingering in the area of the stables was not a good idea but to Daniel it seemed much longer. With one last sweeping glance across the moor, he disappeared into the yard. Soon there was the sound of an engine and the truck came into view once more. From his hiding place, Daniel watched with relief as the vehicle disappeared round the first bend of the lane. He listened until the throbbing of its engine grew fainter and fainter until, finally, he could hear it no more!

The biscuits and the apples looked good. He'd forgotten how hungry he was! Thirsty too! Daniel wondered if he dared go back to the yard. There was a tap there. He'd noticed that on his way to the moor. He would risk it. Riley wouldn't dare to return – at least, not yet. One drink - that would be all he would need and then he would find Ina and Billy. He could tell them everything and they would know what to do! They always knew what to do! Climbing down through the branches, Daniel eased his way towards the ground. It was mossy underfoot and he felt himself slip. His foot twisted underneath him but it was nothing; he'd had much worse in the playground, many a time. He was fine! Clambering to his feet and dusting himself down, he rubbed his ankle and then he froze. The undergrowth directly beneath the tree, disturbed as he'd reached the ground, had parted under his weight to reveal the unmistakable outline of a grey metallic fin.

For what seemed like an age, he couldn't move. Despite the warmth of the afternoon sun, he felt as cold as ice. At last, bending down, he slowly peeled the moss further back just to check – just to be sure. As expected – numbers – chalk- white numbers stencilled on the side. He'd heard Uncle Barney talking about the air raids, telling him about the bombers flying home from their raids on the shipyards. Sometimes they still had bombs in their racks. They would often dump these as they made for open water and home. It was just your luck if your house happened to be underneath one of them. Mostly, the bombs landed on the open countryside that encircled the town. Houses were few and far between up here in the hills and so the fields themselves were peppered with deep craters. Sometimes bombs failed to explode. Uncle Barney had told him all about it. They could lie hidden for years – waiting! Years later, people died. One minute a farmer could be ploughing his field and the next minute he'd be gone!

Daniel stepped backwards and then, slowly and holding on to low branches to steady himself, he worked his way towards the edge of the thicket and the open moor beyond. He knew what to do. All the children knew. Miss Deacon had rehearsed it many times! He had to find an adult and tell and he had to put as much distance between himself and the bomb as possible!

Reaching the gate by the cattle grid, Daniel stopped. He looked back towards the trees. They looked different now. A trap! He slumped down by the gate. Tired! He was tired, very tired. His legs felt like jelly. Sitting down on a patch of bare earth close to the fence, he leaned back against the wooden railing. His mouth was parched. That was when he realised! He'd left his rucksack behind him in the trees! He would have to go back. He had no choice! Just a few more minutes. He could do it. It wasn't far away! Just a short distance! That was when he heard the sound of an engine - loud and clear!

Turning towards the approaching sound, he could make out a vehicle. It was coming towards him. Struggling to his feet, he tried to run but his legs gave way and, as the world finally faded from view, somewhere, in the distance, a dog barked and then there was silence. Daniel closed his eyes and the dark came.

Chapter 9

Ina

Ina returned to her post by the window. She was pretty
sure that she'd heard the sound of a vehicle in the
lane. Billy had been gone since first light and she'd
found it impossible to settle since he'd cycled off towards
the town. All morning, she'd been up and down out of
her chair, jumping at every sound, peering out of the
cottage window, hoping for news. There should have been
something by now!

It was only an old jeep, probably belonging to the
farmer who'd driven past earlier in the day. She'd felt sorry
for the three collies struggling to keep their feet in the
trailer. Whoever was in the driving seat, he hadn't been
away for long. Perhaps he'd forgotten something.

Throwing open the window, she leaned out to see if

the dogs were still aboard. She couldn't see much but Ina was pleased to hear them barking. That was a good sign! The jeep thundered past but then she heard it come to a sudden stop a few yards further along the lane just before reaching the metal cattle grid at the edge of the moor. Ina leaned further out in an effort to see what was happening and was able to make out that the driver had jumped down from the cab and set off at a run across the open ground. The dogs were still barking but made no move to follow. Intrigued, Ina tried to get an even better view but it was quite impossible to see clearly from where she was standing; an overgrown ivy blocked her view. A few minutes passed. No more. The dogs fell silent. Whatever the fuss was about was anybody's business. She heard the jeep being driven off again up the rough track that led on to the moor. Probably a sheep on its back! They did that sometimes, rolled over and then got stuck because of the weight of the fleece. If they weren't turned back on to their feet, they could founder and die but Ina was under the impression that they had all been sheared by now. She'd noticed some when the colonel had shown them round. They hadn't looked particularly woolly! Still, there was more to think about than sheep! She would let the farmer worry about them.

Ina turned back towards the kitchen and put the kettle on. A hot cup of tea might help and making it would pass the time. Staring out of the window was not going to bring Billy back any sooner and it wasn't going to help anyone to find Daniel. By now, he could be anywhere! She had no idea where he could have gone and no-one else seemed to have any idea where he was, either.

The kitchen, like the rest of the cottage, looked like a glossy photograph in a magazine; it was modern and sparkling, with nothing out of place. It looked unused. Colonel McPhee had told them that his daughter, Marianne, worked in London but liked to visit Glenderrin whenever she could so that she could help him with the big house and, of course, help with the horses. He'd beamed with pride when he'd told Ina and Billy what a fine rider she was. He'd taken them to see the rosettes she'd won. They were all pinned up in the tack room for all to see.

Several paintings, delicate watercolour landscapes, were arranged around the walls of the sitting room. Ina spent some time looking at them. Mostly, they were signed by Marianne, herself. Clearly, Colonel McPhee's daughter had other talents beside her skill with horses. Smiling to herself, Ina remembered that, in years gone by, there had been another gifted artist in the McPhee family. It seemed that Marianne had inherited her aunt's talent. Over the fireplace, hung a large painting of a group of Romany children, running along beside a painted caravan. Ina didn't need to look at the signature to know who had painted that! Sadly, the picture turned her thoughts towards her own home, hers and Billy's, now lost forever in the flames and she turned away.

After the fire, the colonel had been quick to take them under his wing and Ina and Billy were indebted to him for that. When her father had telephoned to tell her what had happened, Marianne had insisted straight away that Ina and Billy move into her cottage and stay for as long as they wanted. People had been very kind. Then, of course, there was Barney but Ina couldn't bring herself to think about all of that! There would be time - but not yet.

When Mitchell, the colonel's driver, had delivered a box of groceries, he'd told Ina and Billy that the telephone at the big house was out of action so it wouldn't be possible for PC Wishart to contact them through Glenderrin House until after the engineers had attended to it. That was a problem as Ina and Billy were desperate for news but Mitchell, in his immaculate chauffeur's uniform, had visited the cottage again before driving off to Edinburgh and had cheered them up by delivering fresh milk and eggs. Ina had at least been able to send Billy off with a good breakfast inside him. With things the way they were, he was going to need all his strength.

Daniel could be almost anywhere by now but why had he disappeared? He was usually such a sensible boy. What had possessed him? Why had he run off like that? Bob Wishart was certain that Esther knew something but, try as he might, PC Bob hadn't been able to get anything out of Esther. Esther's lips had been sealed. Pressed by her frantic mother to stop being silly and answer the constable's questions, she'd wept buckets until Bob had felt obliged to help dry her down with one of his best hankies. Mrs Wishart had not been pleased!

Ina poured her tea and cupped the hot beaker in both hands. It was comforting. Absent-mindedly, she wandered out into the back garden with her dog, Alfie, at her heels. Alfie had taken an immediate liking to his new surroundings. Surrounded by the exciting sounds and smells of the countryside, he was in clover! The garden, like the cottage, was a sanctuary. Alfie had made himself at home straight away.

One patch had been planted with purple heather and here Ina paused to sip her tea and watch the bees at work among the flowers. Busy bees! There were bound to be hives somewhere on the moor so there would have to be honey. She would have to find out who the beekeeper was. Billy loved honey on his morning toast. They'd often sat on the steps of the caravan watching the bees in the honeysuckle by the canal. Ina brushed aside a tear that suddenly rolled down her cheek. Hastily, she wiped the back of her hand on her apron. The caravan was gone and that was that; they would have to move on; they'd done it before. This was nothing compared to the camps. They'd survived the camps so they could survive anything.

Keeping to the path that led to the front of the cottage, Ina cast an eye over the plants and stopped to watch a pair of dancing butterflies, Painted Ladies, she felt sure. It was important, somehow, to keep her mind occupied and leave things to Billy. If anyone could find Daniel, he would be the one! She was sure of that but then there was Barney! No, she was not going to think about Barney, not yet! She had to keep a clear head and she had to keep calm. She was going to be needed. Her time would come. She just had to hope that she would be able to find the right words. Barney had asked for her help and she would not be found wanting! Barney was right. He usually was. The time had come. It was only right that Daniel should know. It was time for straight talking but first Daniel would have to be found.

Lost in thought, Ina suddenly found herself wandering out into the lane. The warmth of the sun was comforting as she turned along the winding track that led towards the moor. Strolling past the empty cottage next door and the stables on her left, she noticed, for the first time, that several ponies were out in the paddock close to Glenderrin House. Nervous of horses, she was glad that the fence was in between! She stopped by the moor gate to listen to the birds and watch the swallows hunting for insects on the wing. She guessed they would have nests in the eaves of the bull boxes that stood beyond the wall.

The wide world beyond the gate beckoned but Alfie, Ina's West Highland terrier, wasn't quite ready to venture too far from the security of the cottage - not yet! With one backward glance towards his mistress, he turned tail and headed for the safety of his new home and the soft sheepskin rug by the hearth.

As she reached the stable yard, Ina noticed that the gate had been left wide open. That seemed odd. Still cradling her beaker of tea in her cupped hands, she took a few cautious steps towards the main stable block. There was no-one about but the main door, like the gate, lay wide open and so Ina, with some hesitation, stepped into the semi-darkness. A large corn bin lay open as did the loose-box directly in front of the door. The stalls in the main stable were also empty but then they would be; the ponies were in the paddock. But – where was Midas? Ina was sure that the golden horse should be in his box. He wasn't in the paddock with the others.

The stable was immaculate but corn was scattered across the floor and the lid of the bin lay on its side next to the door of the office. Ina peered around her and called out but there was no reply. Something was wrong!

Ina knew all about the golden horse. Midas's fame went before him and, despite her preference for smaller animals, she was disappointed by the absence of the colonel's favourite. Sipping the last of her tea as she went, Ina turned back towards the door. She shouldn't be here at all. This was, after all, private property. A notice by the gate had made this clear.

Turning to leave, she stopped suddenly as she heard the sound of angry voices and heavy footsteps approaching at speed. A shadow fell across her path and two men filled the doorway. One of them was large and thick-set, the other smaller. Both were out of breath as if they had been running.

"What d'you think you're doing? This is private property!" The menace in the man's voice was unmistakable.

"I'm sorry. I know I shouldn't be here," she replied. "I realise the stables are private but I'm afraid I'm naturally inquisitive and couldn't pass an open door. Actually, I was a bit concerned that the gate was lying wide open and I wondered if something was wrong. My name is Ina, Ina Smith. I'm staying at the the colonel's cottage, just for now, with my husband, Billy. Our caravan was burned down. You may have heard about it. The colonel was very kind and took us in. Do you work here? Do you work for Colonel McPhee? He has been a tower of strength for Billy and myself!"

There was no response, no immediate reply. Then, without a word, the taller of the two men pushed past Ina. He raked an enormous hand through the corn in the open bin, while casting an anxious eye over the scattered grains on the floor; the other man, the smaller of the two, took one frantic look around him and then ran back into the deserted yard.

"Have you seen anybody hanging about here?" demanded the larger man. "You didn't see a boy or a loose horse by any chance?"

"A boy?" Ina tightened her grip on the beaker in her hands. "No. I saw no-one. I haven't seen anyone since early morning, certainly not a boy. Mitchell, the colonel's driver, very kindly brought us some milk and eggs, then some time this afternoon I heard a large vehicle in the lane. A truck, perhaps? It stopped for a while and then I heard it driving off again. There was nothing else." Then she remembered! "Wait!" she added, "I do remember something else! The farmer from up on the hill went past in his jeep and then came back some time later. I'm sure that's right. There were three sheepdogs in the trailer. He wasn't gone for long before he was back and then, for some reason, he stopped near the cattle grid. There was definitely something going on but I couldn't see exactly what it was. He went off to attend to something on the moor. I guessed that one of his sheep had got into difficulty or something like that. He must be back home by this time. If it's the colonel's horse you're worried about, if you think someone's taken it, he might be able to help. You never know - he might have seen something. Maybe you should ask him."

The shorter of the two men returned. "It's gone. Nowhere to be seen!" he growled. "Loose on the moor! Hoof prints in the mud by the gate and other prints besides. Riley was right! There was a boy! That's for sure. You can see where he's been. He's got the horse!"

"And he's been at this!" shouted the other man, pointing towards the open corn bin. His eyes were wild, his face red with anger.

The men paid no further attention to her but, as they turned towards the moor and the stony path that led up to the farm, Ina stiffened. She watched as they both broke into a lumbering run, swaying and stumbling as they covered the uneven ground. There was no hesitation; placing her empty mug on the floor by the open corn bin, she followed. Something told her that where they were going, she should follow.

Progress was slow on the steep path, especially in Ina's fine boots; they were not intended for hill-walking. Struggling to keep the two men in view, she left the pathway and took to the grass. It was rough; patches of ferns and bracken made for difficult progress but it was still softer for her feet. Here and there were patches of damp mud. She tried to avoid those. Soon the two farmhands were out of sight. All she could do was keep going. The sheep farm must be near, somewhere up ahead. She had to be going in the right direction.

When she'd been younger, Ina had walked for miles but now, on challenging ground and an unforgiving incline, she found herself struggling for breath. She had to stop. Her heart was beating faster, so fast that she sat down on a rock by the edge of the path. It was no good; she would have to wait until the throbbing in her chest had settled down. Age was catching up with her. She had to be sensible.

Taking the opportunity to look around her, Ina saw that Marianne's cottage was now far below; she'd travelled further uphill than she'd thought. Remembering that she'd left both doors unlocked, it crossed her mind that she ought to go back. Alfie would be wondering where she'd got to. No, she'd have to risk it and take a chance. In this lonely place, it was unlikely that anyone would pass this way very often. She had to keep going. Somewhere up ahead they'd said there was a boy.

To her left was the moor. It stretched as far as the eye could see, dotted with sheep, grazing and unconcerned. Perhaps a golden horse was out there too, somewhere beyond the horizon. She decided not to think about that. A crow flapped and shifted in the trees, its black wings clipping the branches as it flew out from the copse and a dark cloud passed in front of the sun, now low in the sky. A chill blast of wind sent grasses waving across the open moor. Ina listened for voices but there were none.

A boy, they'd said. It couldn't be Daniel – not here! How would he know where they were? It had all happened so quickly. They'd had no time to prepare themselves let alone tell anyone else what was happening. If it hadn't been for Barney... but there would be time for all that when they found Daniel! Could this boy on the moor be Daniel? He was a resourceful boy. Ina was sure of that. Could he have found them after all? She had to know! She had to keep going! As the brow of the hill approached, she found herself slowing. It had been a steep climb. Up ahead she could see a fence and several beehives. She had known there would be bee hives somewhere here. The hives should mean that the farm was close at hand. She was right. As the steading came into view, she could hear voices and they were raised in anger.

The two men were now only a few feet away from the front door of a large stone farmhouse. They were shouting at a short, stocky figure in brown overalls who was wielding a shotgun! "Get off my land and don't come back!" he was shouting, driving his point home by firing the gun into the air! Three collies were at his heels. Stirred into action by the gunshot, the dogs spread out, fixing their eyes on the retreating targets of their master's fury. A silver dog, larger than the other two, seemed intent on harrying the men down the stony pathway, enthusiastically nipping at their heels all the while. Hurling abuse as they ran, the retreating farmhands were intent only on escape but suddenly, to their relief, they realised that their pursuers were turning their attention elsewhere!

Ina froze as the dogs caught sight of her. She was level with the beehives now and close to the farm. The silver dog advanced as if herding sheep; the others spread out and, keeping close to the ground, began to move towards her. Their eyes were fixed on her face, on her eyes. Ina was fond of dogs but she was afraid. Something told her not to move.

A shrill whistle from the farmer stopped his dogs in their tracks and sent them scurrying back to his side. Hurrying towards Ina, he signalled to her to stay where she was. Although still firmly in his grip, his shotgun was now safely pointing towards the ground. Ina was thankful for that! As he came nearer, she could smell whisky. The man certainly wasn't drunk but the alcohol on his breath was a probable explanation for the reckless driving she'd witnessed earlier in the lane.

"Are you Ina?" The question took her by surprise. The overalls were now in front of her and she could see that inside them was a rosy-cheeked man with a handlebar moustache and a mass of wild grey hair, on top of which was perched a checked cloth cap. He was looking at her intently and looked as puzzled as she was. He waved the gun, rather wildly she thought, in the general direction of the fast-disappearing men from the stables.

"Don't pay any attention to those two layabouts," he growled. "They won't be coming back in a hurry!"

"How do you know my name?" Ina asked.

"Well, I've picked up a lad from the moor. He's asking for Ina and Billy. I reckon you can't be Billy!"

Ina was already moving towards the farm. "It must be Daniel," she cried. "It has to be Daniel! We've been searching everywhere for him and all the time he must have been looking for us!"

The dogs made way, almost as if they knew by instinct not to get caught up in Ina's advance. She didn't stop at the front door. With the farmer at her heels, she burst through the open doorway, calling Daniel's name! There was no answer. Stopping in the hallway, she turned to her companion. Which way to go? There were several doors – several possibilities.

"He's in the kitchen." Her companion pointed to the door on her left, pushing it wider. "Just go in. He's on the settee, half asleep!"

In front of the empty grate, was a couch that had seen better days; a woollen rug had been thrown aside and a cast off cushion lay tumbled on the stone floor. Of Daniel there was no sign but an open window told its tale.

Chapter 10

Run!

Daniel hadn't hesitated. The open window made for an easy exit but, once on the ground, he hadn't dared to lift his eyes; missing his footing on the rough moorland would have meant disaster and yet he knew there was nothing for it now but to run and so that was what he did.

Somehow, these two must have worked things out, worked out that he'd taken the horse. Perhaps Riley had seen him! He'd wondered about that. Worse still, if Birdie and Midge knew about the horse then they'd probably have a good idea that he also had the colonel's money. They'd know what that meant, guess he'd heard them in the yard, that he knew everything and that he could tell! They'd want to put a stop to that!!

Mr Ferguson had been kind. Daniel had opened his eyes to find himself wrapped in a rough travelling rug, a cushion tucked under his head. The old sofa in the farm kitchen had been guarded by three watchful sheepdogs and a gentle old man, who was anxiously bending over him. A hot drink of strong tea and some porridge with honey had revived him so that he was able to explain that he was trying to find his friends, Ina and Billy. He hadn't mentioned the horse or what was in his rucksack and, at least for the moment, he'd decided to say nothing about what lay half-buried in the moss under the trees. He'd decided that the bomb could wait. After all, it had lain there since the war, since a German pilot on his way home from a raid on the shipyards had released his deadly load. If he could only find Ina and Billy, they'd know what to do. Uncle Barney would certainly know how to get help with an unexploded bomb. He'd done that before. He'd told Daniel about it many times. However, at least for now, Uncle Barney was out of reach, far beyond Daniel's reach, at least.

Mr Ferguson had said he could call him Gus. "Most people round here call me that," he'd said with a smile, pushing his well-worn cap to the back of his head. "My real name's Donald but nobody calls me that these days."

A loud knocking had brought their conversation to a sudden end. Gus, with his dogs by his side, had gone to answer the door, leaving Daniel alone in the kitchen. Listening from behind the door, Daniel had heard everything. The voices had been loud, angry and unmistakable and had sent him scrambling through the only exit in sight. There had been no way of knowing what Gus would do on hearing about the horse. He'd been as sure as he could be that Birdie and Midge would say nothing about the missing money. No doubt about that! He'd also been in no doubt that, delivered into their hands, he would have received no mercy. Gus was an old man; he would be no match for Birdie and there was no knowing what tale Birdie and Midge would spin. If Gus believed that Daniel had done something wrong, he might hand him over. Daniel couldn't risk that.

The copse had been further away than he'd thought but he'd known that he had to get there. He'd known that he had to be out of sight before they started back down the path, known that from the crest of the hill he would be in plain sight. Now, finally, in the shelter of the trees, he could pause for breath and take a quick look back towards the farm. Gus had shown his metal and, despite his age and small stature, had, with the additional aid of an ancient shotgun, sent Birdie and Midge packing. Now, angrier than ever, they were heading downhill and in his direction. They'd left the track and were cutting across the grassland. Birdie was in front and pointing towards the trees with Midge following closely behind. Of Gus, there was now no sign.

There was no choice. There was no cover on the open moor. He would have to head for the copse. Trying not to think about how close he was to the bomb, Daniel squeezed between the trees, pushing the undergrowth to one side and treading as softly as he could on the sharp pine needles under his feet.

The grey fin was clearly visible now. Despite the pounding of his heart, he had to press on. His old rucksack lay just where he'd left it at the foot of the tree and just inches away from the bomb itself but this was no time for hesitation. Lifting the bag carefully with trembling fingers, Daniel took aim and tossed it as high up into the tree as he could. His first attempt failed and the bag came crashing down at his feet, missing the bomb by inches. The ground cover of pine needles, leaves and moss helped to muffle the sound. He tried again. At his second attempt the bag, with its precious load, snagged on a branch high in the fork of the tree and stayed put. Success!

The sound of angry voices told him that Birdie and Midge were now heading straight for the trees, straight towards him! They must have seen him or guessed where he would look for a hiding place. Now he had to put as much distance as he could between himself and the money. Birdie and Midge had almost reached the trees. If they were to go searching in the thicket, they would only need to look up and the rucksack would be in full view. If they didn't notice the bomb and went blundering into the undergrowth... Daniel didn't want to think about that. In addition, he didn't want to think about what might happen to him if he fell into their hands. Once again, he had to run for it and hope for the best!

Daniel had barely reached the open moor before Birdie was on him, seizing the collar of his jacket and forcing him to the ground. At first, Daniel managed to slip free but only for a brief moment before he was stopped in his tracks by Midge, who, close on Birdie's heels, proved to be stronger than he looked. There was no escape.

"Where is it?" Birdie demanded. Midge tightened his grip. "We've no time for beating about the bush," continued Birdie, "The only thing likely to get a beating round here is you, so speak up, gypsy. Where is it?"

Midge was quick to join in. "We don't like Romanies round here so make sure you tell us what we want to know. We know you took the horse – horsetail not enough for you these days? You'll pay for that all right - but we're more interested in what else you've helped yourself to!"

Daniel's time on the road had served him well. Despite a quick wash at Kitty's, he still looked scruffy and his hair hadn't seen a comb for some time! Clearly, these two thought they'd caught one of the gypsy lads from Green Lane. He was quick-witted enough to turn that to his advantage.

"Touch me and you'll be sorry," he cried. "A Romany curse is hard to break!" Birdie gave a loud laugh, a laugh that was full of menace. Curses followed – but of a different kind!

"We know how to deal with gypsies. After last year, I'm surprised you dare show your faces round here! I thought I'd fixed you for good!" Birdie dragged Daniel from Midge's grasp and pinned him to the ground. "Now, let's not waste any more valuable time! We can talk about the horse later. For now, let's talk about the money. We know you took it. Where is it? Speak up or it'll be the worse for you!" Winded, Daniel struggled to regain his feet but it was hopeless. Birdie was too strong.

"He was in those trees," shouted Birdie, turning to look at Midge, "Look in there and be quick about it before old Fergie starts pushing his nose in!"

In horror, Daniel watched as Midge disappeared into the copse. He tried to call out – tried to make him stop – but no sound would come. In his dreams, sometimes, when he saw the train, he would open his mouth and try to shout to his father, try to make him stop, try to warn the driver in the cab, try to stop his father from jumping down, try to make him turn back but no sound would come. The words would stick in his throat. It was like that now. No sound would come.

There was no warning! What happened next was as big a surprise to Daniel as it was to anyone else. A small but deadly white missile came flying out of nowhere, a furry ball of air-borne fury, teeth bared and ready for battle! Alfie! Never having thought of himself as a small dog, Alfie had the courage and tenacity of most terriers and was fearless in the face of danger. Having successfully launched himself in the direction of Birdie, he found the strength to sink sharp, determined teeth into the muscular arm that pinned Daniel to the ground. The attack benefited from the element of surprise and was accompanied by a ferocious growling that made it clear that Alfie was far from happy to see a friend in trouble. He was angry enough for anything and anyone and, having seized his quarry, was in no hurry to let go!

Daniel seized the moment to wriggle free and, using the natural slope of the ground to his advantage, rolled clear of his assailant's grasp. His chief concern then was for

Alfie. "Alfie! Alfie!" he cried. The terrier, however, was not about to release his victim without one more satisfying bite, inflicting a painful nip to Birdie's grasping fingers before racing to join Daniel in his flight. Midge, hearing the skirmish, had turned back to lend a hand. He and Birdie were now in furious pursuit.

The sheep took flight! A dog loose on the moor! Daniel knew what could happen to loose dogs among sheep. He turned back to scoop up a wriggling Alfie. That was his undoing! Gripping Daniel by the shoulder, Birdie was not about to be on the receiving end of Alfie's temper. Avoiding the terrier's snapping jaws, he yelled at Midge to grab the dog while he dealt with the boy. This time there would be no wriggling free! This time he would have answers.

"Right! This time we'll have answers and then we'll decide what to do with you and this vicious floor mop." Various adjectives were applied to Alfie as Birdie took a moment to survey the teethmarks on his arm and fingers. Midge was doing his best to keep Alfie from inflicting more damage, this time on him. A streak of blood on Midge's right hand suggested that Alfie had by no means given up the fight. Wriggling and clawing at Midge's overalls, he was desperately trying to free himself but to no avail. Midge was having none of it!

"Don't hurt him!" shouted Daniel as loudly as he could. "He belongs to some friends of mine. If he's on the moor, they must be here too. They'll be here any minute. You'll see! Let me go – or it'll be the worse for you!" Birdie clapped a grimy hand over his mouth. Midge, struggling to restrain Alfie, was beginning to panic.

"We'd better get him back to the yard." His voice was an urgent whisper. 'If old Fergie hears him, we're going to have more problems! For all we know, this could be one of his gypsy pals." Birdie, taking this advice on board, began dragging Daniel in the general direction of Glenderrin. Daniel struggled to keep his feet as the ground sloped away beneath him.

A gunshot from the direction of the farm made Birdie loosen his grip and a second shot, closer now, announced the arrival of two running figures. The first, Gus, brandishing his shotgun, was making surprisingly rapid progress across the rough ground while the second, slower and less sure-footed, was struggling to catch up.

"Daniel! Daniel!"

Alfie wriggled free from Midge's grip and raced across the grass towards the familiar voice. He'd known that Ina was somewhere out here in this wild and unexplored place and now he'd found her! The rocky outcrops and the clumps of rough moorland grasses were nothing to him! He flew, his eager paws hardly touching the ground! Barking with joy, he leapt into Ina's thankful arms.

For Daniel, time stood still and in this frozen moment he knew that he would be safe, that his search was over. He hadn't found Ina. After all, somehow, Ina had found him! He saw her bend to take hold of Alfie, saw her wave to let him know that she was coming, saw her running as best she could. She was coming closer with every step, closer to him, closer to the two farmhands, who stood like statues, their eyes fixed firmly on Gus's shotgun, which was now pointing in their direction but, with every step towards him, Ina and Gus were also coming closer and closer to something else! With every stride, they were coming closer to the bomb under the trees.

"Stop! Stop!" he cried, waving desperately at Ina and Gus. "Stay away! You must stay back!"

Gus had no intention of stopping. He covered the ground with practised ease, his dogs running on ahead. Their piercing eyes never left Birdie and Midge. Low to the ground, they silently circled the two men as if cornering wayward sheep. Following their master's whistle, they dropped to the ground and lay still, awaiting his instructions. Their sharp eyes never left the two men and they were ready!

Shotgun in hand, Gus strode towards Birdie and Midge, his weathered face now red and contorted with rage. Signalling to Daniel to move out of the way, he aimed his gun and his anger at the two men, who, wisely, made no attempt to speak or to move a muscle. They knew when they were beaten!

"What's going on here?" There was no immediate reply. Gus repeated his question. "What's going on? Speak up!" Birdie was the first to find his tongue. Midge simply moved closer to his partner in crime, keeping just behind him and in his shadow, hanging on his every word and nodding in unspoken agreement whenever he thought he should. His eyes lingered on the shotgun.

Birdie launched into a tirade directed initially towards Gus. "Stop waving that gun around before somebody gets hurt! This gypsy's been in the stables while we've been in town; he's taken the colonel's best horse and set the thing loose on this moor. He says not but we know it was him. He was spotted. He's coming with us to find that horse or it'll be the worse for him when the boss gets back! He takes a dim view of gypsies!"

Ina arrived in time to hear everything. Putting an arm around Daniel's shoulders, she protested his innocence.

"Rubbish!" she cried. "For a start, this boy's no gypsy. He's a friend of mine. I know him very well and I can tell you he would never steal anything. There must be some mistake!"

Midge looked at Birdie and, for a moment, Birdie looked lost for words but the silence didn't last for long; he was quick to recover himself. "I don't see any other boy on this moor but I suppose it could've been someone else," he muttered between clenched teeth, "so we'll take your word for it - for now! Could've been a case of mistaken identity, I suppose! Call it a day! No harm done!" His eyes told a different story as he cast a warning glance in Daniel's direction. It was a look that said that their business was not concluded, a look that warned him to keep his mouth firmly shut! With Midge in tow, Birdie turned back towards the moorland track that led down the hill towards Glenderrin.

Daniel took a deep breath! There could be no going back! "It isn't a mistake!" he shouted after the retreating figures of Birdie and Midge. "I may not be a gypsy but I *did* let MIdas out! He's out here on the moor! I did it to keep him safe from you."

Daniel turned towards Gus. "I was coming to find Ina and Billy and I heard these two in the yard. I heard them say that someone called Riley was coming to take the horse away this afternoon. He was to be put in a truck and loaded on to the Irish Boat. Riley was to leave money under the corn bin for them so they could go off to Australia. I heard it all. The colonel would never have seen his horse again. I waited until they'd gone and then I set the horse loose. If things went wrong, Riley was to kill him. They laughed about him being turned into dog meat!"

In stunned silence, Ina simply stared at Daniel as she tried to make sense of things. It was Gus who took charge. He had lowered his shotgun but now he raised it once again, both barrels pointing towards Birdie. Midge looked as if he might take to his heels but, in the end, he stood frozen to the spot, his eyes turned towards Birdie. Birdie would know what to do. Birdie would know. He always knew what to do. Birdie would get them out of this. He'd got them out of tight corners before! He would leave Birdie to do the talking!

'Well?" demanded Gus, "What have you got to say for yourselves?"

It was, as anticipated, Birdie who spoke. "Sounds like a load of rubbish to me," he sneered. "He's been reading too many comics. He's made it all up!"

Midge found his voice: "You can't prove any of this. Just your word against ours. You're just a kid – and you've admitted taking the horse – in front of witnesses!"

Birdie glared at him. "Leave this to me!" But it was too late!

"I *can* prove it," Daniel cried. "They took a lot of money as well, money belonging to the colonel! It was in the safe in the big house. They tried to make me tell them where it is – but I didn't! If you hadn't come along, they were going to make me show them where it's hidden. It's in a safe place so we can give it back to Colonel McPhee! I'm the only one who knows where it is."

It was Gus who now looked puzzled, struggling to make sense of everything that Daniel had said but he kept the two men steadfastly in his sights. There was real danger in the air. The sheepdogs felt it and had raised themselves as if ready to spring, their keen eyes fixed on Birdie and Midge, their trained ears waiting for their master's call. The silver grey collie with the wall eye curled its lip in an enthusiastic snarl.

"Steady!" warned Gus. "Lie down!" Reluctantly, the dogs obeyed. "What are we talking about here?" asked Gus, without taking his eyes off the two farmhands. "How much money exactly?"

Daniel gave him the answer he sought. "They stole a thousand pounds. They want it so they can buy a place in Australia."

"He's mad!" shouted Birdie. " He's making the whole thing up. It's nonsense. The colonel's safe is always locked and only the colonel knows the combination. We're in the clear so, if he's got some money, he must have taken it himself!"

Gus hesitated, not sure how to proceed. Everything was becoming very complicated! Daniel tried to remember anything that might help. They were right. It would be difficult to prove that they were the ones who'd taken the money. They could just deny everything.

"They do know the combination of the safe and so do I now! It's to do with the horse's height!" Daniel continued. "It's 172172! I heard them talking about it! You can check with the colonel."

He paused to let this piece of information sink in and then went on. "They left the stolen money in the corn bin. I found it when I dug out some corn for Midas". Then he remembered something else! "They were going to pick it up when they came back from the market. They were going to put all the money together and take it to somewhere called Mandalay!"

"But Mandalay isn't in Australia," said Ina. 'It's in -"

"Burma!" Gus finished her sentence. "Or is it?" he added, staring hard at the two men.

Birdie and Midge looked cornered. Fear was in their eyes. Gus fixed them with an unrelenting gaze. "I know now, without a shadow of doubt, that this boy is speaking the truth," he continued. "We all know that now, don't we? What's more, the colonel will know it too!"

The two men made no reply. For a split second it appeared as if they might run but, after a nervous glance towards the three eager collies, they decided against it. They looked beaten.

"I don't understand," Ina said softly.

Gus did not for one moment take his eyes off the two farmhands. His expression spoke of anger and disgust. "The colonel was a far-travelled man in his day," he explained. "He spent several years in Burma – met his wife there. Out of sentiment, he named the cottages after places they'd visited together. The cottage you're in at present, the one that's owned by Marianne, the colonel's daughter, is called 'Rangoon' and the other, the one next door that's lying empty, is 'Mandalay' - the ideal place for someone to hide some stolen money, don't you think? No-one ever goes in there. The cottages' name boards rotted away long ago and the colonel never got round to replacing them after his wife died. There's no way this lad could have known anything about that – no way he could have made the connection with Mandalay. These two are guilty all right and they know that they've been found out fair and square!"

"What now?" Cunning in the face of defeat, Birdie was saying very little. He would wait to see which way the wind would blow.

"You'll have to give me a moment to think about that," replied Gus," but make sure you keep very still while I'm thinking!"

Suddenly, the collie dogs rose to their feet, their eyes turned as one towards the open moor. Even Alfie was transfixed. In the distance, but getting closer with every step, was a horse, a horse that, in the closing rays of the afternoon sun, seemed to be made of shimmering gold.

Chapter 11

Truth to Tell

His coat shining in the evening sun, his head nodding as he covered the sloping ground, Midas was not alone. He was being led by a tall, wiry lad of about thirteen while a smaller boy, mounted bareback, held on to the horse's mane. The older boy waved.

"We found him on the moor," he shouted, a broad grin evident even at a distance. "It's Midas!"

Gus called back but his shotgun remained steady and aimed in the general direction of Birdie and Midge. "Well! Well! Would you believe it! It's my good friends from Green Lane, Ned and Jacob, and just look at what they've found!"

Keeping an unflinching eye on Birdie and Midge, Gus signalled to his dogs to be still and waited in silence as the two boys approached. Daniel noticed that the older boy was carrying what appeared to be a shepherd's crook in his left hand. With his right he steered the horse towards the copse and the watchers on the hillside. As they came nearer, Daniel could see that the boys were very much alike. He guessed they must be brothers.

"Well done, lads!" said Gus, as they stopped beside him. "You've done a good job to-day and I'll make sure the colonel gets to know all about it! Where did you find him?"

"He was down in the hollow by the burn," replied the older boy. "He was in the gorse near the stile. We were over there checking on a ewe that was fast in the brambles and he just walked over to us - easy as pie! We knew it was the colonel's horse straight away but we guessed he shouldn't be loose on the moor so we fetched him home. Thought there might be some good money in it!"

Gus continued to keep his shotgun trained on the two men but permitted himself a wry smile.

"You were right," he said. "More money than you might think!" Reaching into his trouser pocket, he pulled out a roll of notes held together with a broad elastic band. "I've been down into the town today collecting my winnings from the Ayr races. Had a few good horses running well for me this week! I think you've earned a share!" Handing the shotgun to Ina, he warned her to keep it pointing towards Birdie and Midge, who looked even more uneasy now that Ina's nervous finger hovered close to the trigger. Slowly, Gus peeled the band from around the banknotes and stuffed two pound notes into the waiting hand of the small boy on the horse.

"Remember, Jacob, it's for sharing, mind!" he added. "Now I'd better pay your wages before you head back to Green Lane or you'll not be turning up tomorrow!" Two more banknotes were produced and this time pressed into the palm of Ned, the older of the two, who was also told to make sure he shared the spoils.

Ned was clearly struggling to keep Midas steady as the horse's sharp ears had picked up the calls of the ponies in the paddock at the bottom of the hill. Midas was ready for home.

"You can leave the crook with me for now but I'll have it ready for you tomorrow morning along with a proper breakfast," said Gus, "and don't forget it's seven o'clock sharp and then we'll see what the colonel has to say about the good day's work you've done today. I'll be surprised if there isn't a bit more cash to be earned out of all of this." The crook was duly returned and, with a sly grin towards the two silent farmhands, the boys turned the horse towards the stables and home. There would be no questions for now. Questions could wait until the morning!

"Just put him in the paddock for now," added Gus. "It's where he wants to be. I'll see to the other jobs later on and the colonel will be back in the morning."

As the boys headed off, Gus called after them, "Well done, lads!" before turning back to deal with Birdie and Midge. Shotgun once again firmly in his hands, and the whiff of whisky still noticeable on his breath, he had their undivided attention.

Ina and Daniel stood close together, Ina with a reassuring arm round Daniel's shoulders. Gus had made up his mind. "The colonel won't want any trouble or gossip about the place so I'm going to give you two a chance – just the one mind!" Gus was in no mood for debate. "If you two are set on Australia, I'm going to do you a favour." His voice was low and steady but he made no attempt to hide his anger.

"Here's what we're going to do! You two are to get your things and clear off right now. I know you've had your wages and that should be enough to see you on your way to Australia and good riddance to the pair of you. If you're prepared to work your passage and prepared to work once you get there, you'll have cash to spare so go and don't come back! If you're still here when the colonel gets home in the morning, it'll be the worse for you. We'll be heading to the polis with all of this. That'll put an end to Australia or anywhere else, for that matter! They don't want criminals these days!I hope I'm making myself clear! If you two are still on the colonel's land in the morning, still here when the colonel gets back, then we go to the fiscal's office with all of this and the lad tells his story to him! He and the colonel are old pals so there won't be any messing about. You two will be behind bars before you can say Botany Bay!"

Birdie and Midge stood in silence. "Make up your minds," growled Gus. "We haven't got all day and my patience is wearing thin! I must be mad to give you two thieving time-wasters any sort of chance at all. Still, if you want to try your luck with the colonel that's your lookout. Oh, and by the way, there's also the possibility that I might have to tell my friends on Green Lane who it was that set fire to that caravan last summer! I don't have any actual proof, of course, which is why I didn't go to the polis at the time, but the Romanies won't need proof. They'll be happy to take my word for it and deal with the matter themselves!"

For once, Midge was the first one to speak. He knew when he was beaten! "Come on, Birdie! Let's go!"

As they turned to go, Gus called after them. "And make sure you tell your friend, Riley, or whatever his name is, not to show his face round here again or I'll set the dogs on him! The dock polis might be glad to know about him and his pal on the Irish Boat. I'll be sure to be having a word with them."

Daniel watched as the two men disappeared in the direction of the big house. They didn't look back. "Do you think they'll really keep their side of the bargain?" asked Ina. Gus frowned. "They'd better," he replied, "because it'll be the worse for them if they hang around here – and they know it! The colonel was about to sack them. He told me as much last week. He's had enough of their idleness. The only reason they've lasted until now is that it's difficult to find good staff these days. People want to work in the town. They don't want to be in service. The big house has been without a cook for three weeks and Mrs Atkins, the housekeeper, is getting on a bit; I think she's planning to move in with her sister. If Colonel McPhee didn't have Mitchell, he'd practically be managing on his own! Mitchell's missus helps out a bit when things get a bit tight but it's not enough."

Turning to Daniel, Gus suddenly looked very serious. "Now, my young friend," he said, "you'd better tell me where this money is." Ina nodded.

Daniel pointed in the direction of the trees. "I threw it up into a tree in there! It's stuck on a branch half-way up."

"Show me where it is and we can get it down," continued Gus. "Unless it's very high, we should be able to free it with this crook." With his dogs at heel, he turned to head for the trees. Ina followed with Alfie in her arms.

"Wait!" shouted Daniel. "You don't understand! It isn't just the money that's in there. There's something else!" Gus and Ina stopped and turned towards him but, as she turned, Ina loosened her grip on the restless Alfie, who took his chance. He couldn't resist the scents and sounds of the copse any longer! Wriggling free, he raced into the undergrowth and disappeared into the dark coolness of the trees. There must be rabbits in there, for sure!

Daniel could only watch in horror! "There's a bomb!" he cried. "In there! There's a wartime bomb! Don't go in!" Ina looked at Gus. This was his territory. Surely he would know what to make of this. She was right.

"The boy could well be right," he said. "We've had a good few of these in the years since the war. Bomb Disposal know their way around this moor! The things keep turning up and causing us problems. I curse the Germans every day of my life!"

Ina looked upset. "There are good German people, you know. I know lots of good German people, lots of good German people! The war is over now."

Daniel said nothing but his face showed where his sentiments lay. The Germans were the enemy, in his book. He didn't know any German people and he had no intention of getting to know any!

Reading Daniel's expression, Ina continued, "Let me tell you something. Billy's Mum and Dad were German and, although I've never told you this before, Billy is German too. He was born in Berlin long before the war and his full name, although no-one has used it for many years, is Wilhelm Schmidt. Billy's father was a clever engineer and he brought his family here to Scotland a long time ago so that he could work in the shipyard. He was a preacher too, like Billy, a good man, a good German man who worked very hard for his family and was a friend to everyone he met."

Daniel was lost for words. Ina was his friend. Billy was his friend. How was it possible that Billy could be German? Ina, however, was intent on saying what she had to say. Now that she had started, she couldn't seem to stop! The words came pouring out as if a dam had burst!

"During the war, Billy and I had to go to a camp – several camps – because Billy was German. We had no-one to speak for us. No-one! We were interned. That's what they called it. It was terrible. We hadn't done anything wrong. We were against the war but we had no choice. Billy was German and so we had to go and, even after the war, even after Billy had changed his name, some people still didn't trust us. Billy has never been able to have a church of his own because some people won't come to hear him preach and some have even spread stories that we were involved with racketeers during the war, which isn't true. We're honest people, Daniel. You know that. You know that Billy is a good man, whatever other people might think or say!" Ina stopped, her voice suddenly fading. She hadn't meant to say quite so much but the words had all come tumbling out – the cruel injustice of it all and the hurt she felt for Billy.

Daniel took Ina's hand and squeezed it. "Billy's a good man," he said," and I'll tell everybody that. Whether he's German or not, I know he's a good man and so does Uncle Barney!" He could see tears in Ina's eyes. It had been a strange day and it wasn't over yet. The sky was darkening and there was a sudden chill in the wind that blustered across the moor. "I'm sorry, Ina," he said, "I didn't know."

Ina and Daniel had forgotten about Gus but, when they finally turned to speak to him, he was no longer there. In silence they waited. Even the dogs huddled together, restless and uneasy. They had watched their master disappear and now they anxiously awaited his return. They didn't have long to wait.

"The boy's right," Gus announced, emerging from the thicket. "It's a bomb and it's a fair size so we need to get right away from this spot! Come on! No more talking!" Gus was already trudging downhill in the direction of the cottages and the stables. Daniel and Ina, with Alfie now safely in her arms, followed close behind. The three sheepdogs ran on ahead, not stopping until they reached the cattle grid. There they paused to look back as if seeking further instructions.

"Lie down!" shouted Gus – and they did. As they reached the cottages, Gus stopped. He leaned the crook against the fence and reached inside his jacket. "You were right about the money, too! It didn't want to leave that tree at first but it was no match for my stick!" Triumphantly, he held Daniel's rucksack aloft.

Daniel had forgotten all about the money in his rucksack. His thoughts had been with Ina and Billy and how unhappy and afraid they must have been, how sad it was that they had been treated so badly because they had a German name. He wondered if Uncle Barney had known this all along and kept it from him. Uncle Barney was certainly keeping something from him but he didn't think that it had anything to do with Ina and Billy. He had a feeling there was something else, something even bigger!

"Now," said Gus, "we have to make sure that this money stays safe until the colonel gets back!" They had reached the garden gate of the cottage but Ina paused, suddenly remembering that, in her eagerness to follow the two farmhands, she had left the cottage door unlocked and lying open. That was how Alfie had been able to make his escape! Seeing her concern, Gus took charge.

"You two wait outside for now," he whispered. A shrill whistle brought his dogs to heal. "I won't go in alone though." For a short time, that seemed much longer, Daniel and Ina waited in silence until, finally, Gus reappeared with a broad smile on his face. "All clear!" he cried and, with obvious relief, Ina and Daniel made their way into the cottage. Alfie, cheerfully raced on ahead.

"Now, we have to make sure that this cottage is locked up tight," instructed Gus. "Lock up as soon as I've gone and make sure that all the windows are fastened. Keep an eye out for those two, although I don't think we'll have any more trouble from them. If they know what's good for them, they'll be packing their bags and making sure they're well away from here as soon as possible." Looking around for a suitable hiding place, his gaze settled on a large sideboard at the back of the room. He pushed the rucksack out of sight behind it.

"Should be safe enough there until the colonel gets back!"

"Where are you going?" asked Ina. She was back to her old self and ready to play her part in whatever needed to be done.

"I'm taking the truck into town to report that bomb. We're losing the light now so Bomb Disposal won't do anything about that until tomorrow but they need to know! They'll be up here at first light!" Almost as an afterthought he added, "I'll let them know down at the polis station that young Daniel here is safe and sound. Half the town'll be looking for him, by now! I'll keep an eye out for that husband of yours while I'm at it!"

Daniel saw Ina turn towards the window. Two figures were hurrying down the lane. Birdie and Midge! They were carrying two holdalls and heading in the direction of the main road. Birdie was in the lead with Midge struggling to keep up. They looked straight ahead, paying no attention whatsoever to the cottages nor to the three faces now keeping watch over their departure.

"I'll let them get on their way before I leave," Gus said. "We don't want them doubling back when they know I've gone."

Minutes later, he was indeed gone and they were alone. The front door was firmly closed and Ina and Daniel stood in the hallway, looking at each other. There was a silence that seemed to fill the cottage. Ina was the first to speak.

"I'm sure you've got a lot to tell me, Daniel and I know that you'll have plenty of questions for me," she said softly, "but first we really do have to find some proper food for you and then, when you've had a good wash and changed into some clean clothes, we can sit down and have a proper talk."

"I haven't got any other clothes to put on," Daniel said lamely. He was suddenly aware of how dirty he was. He was tired too.

"Your spare clothes are here. They're on the bed upstairs," Ina replied. She was smiling. "Pam from Welfare helped PC Wishart to sort them out and Bob brought them up here for us. You were to stay with us while Barney was in hospital."

"Hospital!" Daniel cried. "Uncle Barney's in hospital?"

"Where did you think he was when you ran away?"

"Prison! Esther said - "

Ina interrupted. "Esther is a sweet girl, Daniel, a lovely girl - but she can get things mixed up. She can get the wrong end of the stick! You should know that by now." She paused. Daniel waited, his eyes searching Ina's face for some reassurance. The sun had set and the lamps had not been lit; in the dim hallway it was difficult to read her expression.

"Is Uncle Barney sick?" he asked. Then he remembered the caravan. "Your caravan! Is this to do with the fire? Is Uncle Barney hurt?"

"You saw the mess and came to find us, I suppose." Ina was beginning to put some of the pieces of the jigsaw together but the picture was still very hazy. "We need to have a talk, Daniel. We should have had one a long time ago. There are things you should have been told by now – important things - but Barney just couldn't find the words. He was afraid. That's what he came to talk to us about that day – the day of the fire. If he hadn't been there..." She paused before continuing. "Barney is safe and well. That's the main thing that you need to know. The rest of the story can wait until later. Before we do anything else, I want you to go upstairs and make yourself respectable. You do look as if you've been dragged through a hedge backwards!" She laughed. "When you come down try to look a bit more like Daniel Abercrombie and later we can have that talk and something to eat. The food should probably come first. I'll set the table while you're getting changed. How about scrambled eggs on toast? I have some lovely fresh eggs that Mitchell brought this morning." Daniel nodded. Scrambled eggs sounded good. His questions could wait. Uncle Barney was safe and he wasn't in prison. Poor Esther! There was going to be a great deal of explaining to do!

Cleaning up took longer than he'd expected. A brave look in the bathroom mirror had shown how desperately a wash was needed! However, the look of smiling approval on Ina's face when she met him at the foot of the stairs on his return told him that he had done a good job!

"Now," she said, "let's get some proper food into you! We can't stand in this hallway all night!"

Suddenly, Ina froze. Placing a finger to her lips, she signalled to Daniel to keep absolutely quiet! Following her gaze, Daniel turned to face the front door. The key was still in the lock. Daniel had watched Ina lock it after Gus had left but now, just outside that door, he could hear exactly what Ina had heard, the unmistakeable sound of approaching footsteps.

At the foot of the stairs stood a brass umbrella stand containing two umbrellas and a sturdy, wooden walking stick. Without a sound, Ina stretched out her right hand and withdrew the larger of the two brollies. This she handed to Daniel. Then, taking hold of the gnarled walking stick, she raised it above her head. Whatever happened next, they were ready!

For a moment, there was just the crunching of two pairs of heavy boots on the gravel path and then the sound of footsteps on the stone steps outside. The door creaked as someone or something began to push it from the other side. As Ina and Daniel watched, the brass door handle slowly began to turn but the door stayed firmly in its place. Muffled voices could be heard but it was impossible to make out what was being said then, slowly, the brass flap of the letterbox began to rise. That was when Ina remembered the back door. She'd left it wide open when she'd wandered into the garden with her mug of tea. She had to hope that Gus had checked it but what if he hadn't?

Chapter 12

Uncle Barney

B arney had always known that some day Daniel would have to be told and that he would have to be the one to tell him. That was how it needed to be, how he wanted it to be but would he be able to do it and would it change everything between Daniel and himself? That was the question that was keeping him awake at nights. In these last few weeks there had been times, several times, when he'd almost got there but he'd held back and said nothing. He'd let the moment pass but Daniel was on to him. He was sure of that. Daniel was not easily fooled. The boy was bright; he knew something was in the air. He couldn't put it off much longer, not now! He just had to hope that when Daniel was safely home, he would find the words, somehow find the courage to tell him and hope that Daniel would be able to forgive him, that he would understand, that they could go on just as before. However, before that Daniel had to be found.

Looking back over these last days brought little comfort and looking ahead wasn't any better. The throbbing in his right hand had begun to ease, which was a relief but his left ankle was still swollen and painful especially when he walked for any distance. The doctor had said that it would be fine in a day or two. He'd said that there was nothing to worry about. It was nothing serious. He'd been very lucky, one way and another. Barney knew what luck could do. It could be good or bad. He had to hope that his good luck would hold fast!.

Barney felt despair when he thought about the boys. It had been a miracle that no-one had been killed. He thought of them as lost souls. Given half a chance, they'd be all right but, with things the way they were, the future didn't look too bright. Some of these boys had lost all their families in the Blitz. They'd lived through the horrors of a war that had landed on their doorsteps. The shipyards and the ordnance factories had been obvious targets for the bombing raids, fire storms that had largely missed their targets but had flattened the town itself. The world they'd known as children had been stolen away but the spirit of the town had risen above the flames and rubble and, despite it all, the work of building the ships and armaments had continued by day and by night.

The children of the town, however, had seen things, dreadful things, that children should never have to witness. For safety, many had been moved to live with relatives far away beyond the hills; some had become refugees, moving from pillar to post in strange places far from their homes, lodging with strangers they had never met before. Now, much older, they struggled to find their feet in a world that that still bore the scars from the ravages of war. Surrounded by the wreckage that war had left behind, they were reminded every day of all that had gone before. The boys, in particular, found safety - of a kind - in numbers, huddling together in their street gangs. Crammed in the prefabs and struggling to find work, they had too much time on their hands. Barney didn't want it to be like that for Daniel – but where was Daniel and why had he run away from the home they shared? Barney remembered the women talking on the stairs. Their whispering voices had carried up the stairwell and he'd heard every word. Had Daniel heard them too? It was an explanation that was hard to ignore but he pushed it to the back of his mind as best he could.

He'd spent hours listening for Daniel's footsteps on the stairs. He'd been in and out so many times, in and out on to the landing, leaning over the bannisters, peering down into the stairwell, listening for any sound that would mean that Daniel's foot was on the stair, that he was safe. All he could hear were the familiar sounds of the terrace itself, mainly the echoing voices of children playing games in the back courts, their laughter rising on the warm, dusty summer air, just the normal sounds of life in Abercrombie Terrace on any warm Saturday afternoon.

It had been a Saturday when he'd heard the women talking far below him, talking in whispers to each other while they took their turn of scrubbing the stairs. The sun had been shining through the skylight high above and it had just seemed like any other day. The women hadn't heard him closing the front door, hadn't known that he'd heard their every word, drifting up through the landings on the warm air. His heart had sunk. He'd always known, of course, that it was just a matter of time before someone said something. It was a miracle that he'd been able to keep it from Daniel for so long. In fact, it said a great deal for his good neighbours on the terrace that he'd been able to keep things from Daniel all this time. They'd kept his secret just as he had and he was grateful for that, very grateful, but walls have ears and, if he could catch shared whispers on the stairs, then it wasn't going to be too long before Daniel did the same. The time had come and he had to be honest, at last. Daniel was growing up, almost ready for the move on to secondary school. He would have to hope that Daniel was old enough to understand but finding the words, finding the right words, was not going to be easy.

Since returning to the flat early that morning, he'd spent a great deal of time listening at the top of the outside stairs, hoping to hear Daniel's footsteps. When he hadn't been leaning over the bannisters and staring down into the stairwell, he'd been in the front room, his weary eyes scouring Abercrombie Terrace for any sign of him. There had been none. Beyond the railway line, he could see the park. Saturday was always a busy day. He knew some of Daniel's haunts there and, despite the ache in his ankle, he had searched them all without success. He'd even climbed the stairs to search behind the stage at the open-air theatre that everybody called "the bandstand". In the end, he'd just had to give up because of the pain and leave the rest of the searching to Billy. Despite his own considerable problems, Billy was still out there, combing the town and making regular checks at the polis station. Billy was a good friend, as was Ina. They had never deserved all that life had thrown at them.

Returning to the terrace empty-handed and exhausted, Barney had tried, without success, to settle in his armchair and get some sleep. They'd wanted him to stay in hospital for one more night but he'd refused. He'd spent two nights there already and, although everyone had been very kind, there was no way he could stay while Daniel was out there somewhere in the dark. Daniel had always been afraid of the dark. The word lingered. Dark! He'd kept Daniel in the dark for too long. It was time for that to end – but first he had to find Daniel and he had no idea where to look.

It was obvious from what he'd been told by Bob Wishart that Esther knew something but that she was determined to say nothing at all. Bob's attempts to extract information from her had merely resulted in floods of tears from Esther, herself, and a rather "put-out" Mrs O'Callaghan, who hadn't minced her words!

"I said you could leave the boy with me," she'd protested. "He would've been fine here with us until Barney came home. It was only going to be for a couple of nights! We would've managed. I told you all that but you wouldn't listen! Oh no!" PC Wishart had been pleased to escape her wrath, especially as he'd spotted a nearby Joshua scratching his head and Mrs O'Callaghan reaching almost absent-mindedly for the fine-tooth comb! The constable's scalp had itched all the way home!

Bob Wishart had been very good at keeping Barney up to date with all that was happening. Every police officer, who could be spared, had joined the search for Daniel, some even offering up their off-duty time to try to find the boy but to no avail. On returning to Abercrombie Terrace, Barney had been met by kindly neighbours bringing scones and home-made soup and anything else they'd thought might help him to "keep his strength up". Paul had sat with him for a while, pacing the floor alongside him, despite his limp, desperately trying to think of the right things to say. In the end, he'd had to go but he'd stayed as long as he could. Paul understood better than most what was running through Barney's mind but, like Barney, he wasn't about to put it into words.

"Try to get some sleep," the doctor had said earlier when Billy had collected him from the ward. "You need to look after yourself. Smoke and canal water are not a good combination. Like your two friends, you've had a nasty shock and you need to give yourself time to get over it!" Barney had nodded in agreement, knowing all the while that there was not much hope of rest for Billy, Ina or himself until Daniel was safely home. They'd caught the tram right outside the hospital and Billy had walked beside him all the way back from the terminus. He'd managed the stairs pretty well but had been glad to reach the top. The doctor had been right after all!

Billy had made a pot of tea for them both but had started by reaching for the wrong teapot, the old one on the mantel, which had led to the discovery that Daniel had taken most of the money with him. Barney hadn't been sure whether that was a good sign or a bad one!

Why exactly had Daniel run off? That was still a puzzle. After the fire, it had been agreed that Ina and Billy could take Daniel to Glenderrin to stay with them until Barney could be discharged from hospital. The colonel had been quick to step in and offer his daughter's cottage to Ina and Billy. That had saved the day. They'd lost everything in the fire.

Given Barney's house key, Pam Stoddart, from Welfare, had agreed to collect Daniel from school at the end of the day. She was to take him safely back to Abercrombie Terrace to pack his things before going on to Glenderrin. PC Bob was to take them there in a polis car. They'd all agreed that Daniel would love that bit! However, a telephone call from a tearful Miss Deacon had put paid to their plans. Daniel was missing!

The headteacher had gathered all the children in the drill hall to find out if anyone had known anything that could help find Daniel. Everyone had looked straight at Esther! Some of the boys had said that they'd seen Daniel talking to Esther O'Callaghan just before he'd disappeared, which had resulted in Esther being questioned at length, first by the headteacher, secondly by Miss Deacon and finally by PC Bob. It had been a long and distressing process that had yielded no information whatsoever. Esther's lips, though they had trembled, had remained sealed! If Esther knew why Daniel was missing or where he could be found, she was determined to keep quiet about it.

All Barney could do now was wait. Billy had waited long enough to ensure that Barney had drunk his tea and then he'd set off again back to town to help with the search. "You need to be here in case Daniel turns up!" he'd insisted.

The trains passed by Abercrombie Terrace all day long - even through the night when the freight trains flew through the stations at express speed. Even when he was asleep Barney could hear them, whether they were there or not. There was no escape from the steam and the whistles and the rumbling of the wheels, all of which he had once loved. Despite the fact that the coal yard was built not very far from the main line, working with the old carthorses and the sturdy little ponies kept him busy in a good way. Ina and Billy had told him many times to move away from the railway, to find somewhere different that wasn't a constant reminder of that day. A bit of him longed to do just that but how could he? Where could they go? Abercrombie Terrace was the only home they had ever known, his and Daniel's.

He'd tried sitting quietly in the Memorial Garden, staring at the bronze plaque that told the story of his brother's bravery but that had proved too hard to bear. He'd read the inscription so many times that he knew it by heart. It told how his brother, "Walter Abercrombie, with no regard for his own safety, jumped from the platform down on to the railway line in a vain attempt to rescue Robert Fairley, aged two years, who had fallen on to the rails." The date was there along with a Latin inscription, the exact translation of which Barney had long since forgotten but he knew what it meant. His brother had died in a brave attempt to save an unfortunate child but it had all been for nothing. Both lives had been lost. His self- sacrifice was celebrated in an ancient tongue, as was his bravery.

The bronze plaque bore the image of a man on the line carrying a small boy in his arms. Barney could hardly bear to look at it. In the background the looming shape of an advancing train could just be seen. Occasionally, he'd taken Daniel to the Memorial Garden. They had sat together and Daniel had read the inscription, looked at the picture and laid a flower by the side of the rockery that old Mr Duff had planted out with plants from his own garden.

The park-keeper was a strange man, something of an outsider, but even he had wanted to do something, something to show his respect. Not good with people, he was more at home with his plants. An old soldier, he'd served in North Africa with the Desert Rats and, on his return, had taken to growing strange and exotic plants that reminded him of his days under African skies. While most of his comrades had hated the desert, Duffy had loved it! He'd often invited Barney to go and see his "jungle garden", as he called it but, somehow, he'd never got round to it. Barney felt guilty when he thought about that. He ought to put that right. Barney had come to the conclusion that, rather like Duffy, he didn't find people very easy. Perhaps a garden would have helped but there wasn't much hope for that on Abercrombie Terrace.

Walter, Barney's brother, had always been the one who was quick to make friends, always the one to see the funny side of everything. Wounded in the war, he'd been invalided out, sent home early. He'd made a good recovery but his back and leg injuries had left him with a limp. If it hadn't been for that bad leg, Walter might have made it back to the platform in time. Barney had often wondered about that.

During the war, like many of the local men and because of his work in the shipyard, Barney had been kept out of the armed forces apart from the Home Guard. He'd enjoyed that – all the marching and training up in the hills! He'd actually made some pals and they'd managed to have many a laugh despite the blackouts, the fire-watching and the air raids. They'd been a team and he'd liked that until the horrors of the Blitz. That had changed everything but still, he told himself, they'd been useful! Barney had always enjoyed sharing his Home Guard adventures with Daniel, who didn't seem to mind that he'd heard the stories several times before – but where was Daniel now? Where was he and what was he doing?

He'd told Daniel about his various jobs, of which there had been many – in the shipyard and at the tank tracks, in the coal yard and, for a short time, in the sewing-machine factory. He'd always been quick to learn new skills. That was the reason they'd asked him to help when they were short staffed on the line. He'd driven the small steam engines in the shipyard so he'd been an obvious choice. Still, he hadn't told Daniel about that. He hadn't told him he'd been an engine driver. He'd never told him that.

Looking back at the last few days, it was easy to see that things had really started to go wrong when he'd been asked to report to Mr Gilligan's office on Wednesday evening after work. There were always lots of deliveries on a Wednesday and so Barney had gone out with one of the carts, as he often had in the past, just to help out. Everything had seemed perfectly normal – just another day! However, at the end of his shift had come the bombshell! Mr Gilligan was to retire. His son, Thomas, who was to take over the business, had decided to change over to motorised trucks for delivering the coal; the horses and ponies were to go to a dairy in the city as the people in the big houses liked the horse-drawn floats and old coal horses were popular because they were reliable in traffic and they didn't mind standing and waiting! Mr Gilligan had explained that competition in the big city was such that the delivery men still used horses, if they could get them, because the customers preferred them. They seemed to make them think about times past and countryside remembered. Sadly, they were not going to need Barney at the yard any more. Mr Gilligan had given him the wages owed to him, had thanked him for all that he'd done and had told him he could take the rest of the week off so that he could begin to look for another job. He'd shaken Barney by the hand and wished him well.

Barney had felt numb. Before leaving, he'd gone round all the stalls and patted each horse and pony in turn. He knew them all by name, knew all their little ways and how they liked to have him scratch behind their ears at the end of a long shift before settling them in for the night. He'd grown to love life at the coal yard and, apart from that, it brought in steady money. It was certainly not going to be easy to find another job at the moment. There would be hard times ahead and there was Daniel to think of. Instead of telling Daniel straight away, he'd kept the news to himself. He'd needed time to think – and then there had been the whispers on the stairs to think of. Life had suddenly become complicated!

On Thursday morning he'd gone out just as usual, as if there was nothing wrong. Daniel hadn't appeared to notice anything. (Barney now wondered if he'd been wrong about that!) With a heavy heart, he'd set off to talk things over with Ina and Billy before telling Daniel. After that, he'd planned to make his way to the Labour Exchange in Riverside.

He'd spotted the lads from the prefabs straight away. They were often hanging about and on the lookout for mischief so he'd kept them in his sights. It had been obvious to Barney that they were watching Billy, who was working on The Wayside Pulpit, writing his message for the day in his perfect copper-plate script and blissfully unaware of the danger. By the time he'd realised what was happening, it had been too late!

Barney had run as fast as he could but by the time he'd reached the caravan it was already alight. A strong smell of petrol had left him in no doubt that this attack, not the first that Ina and Billy had suffered, was much more serious than anything that had gone before. Cruel rumours about Billy and Ina had often caused problems for them in the past. Lies that Billy had been involved with racketeers during the war had succeeded in making them outcasts. People were suspicious because Billy came from a German family and that made him an enemy despite the fact that he was the kindest man that Barney had ever known.

Barney had helped Billy to pull Ina and Alfie out of the van before attempting to tackle the blaze but it had proved to be a hopeless task. The wooden caravan had made excellent kindling and the fire had rapidly taken hold. It must have been at that point that the boys had realised that things had gone too far; they hadn't meant it to be like this; it had all got out of hand. One of them, in an act of desperation, had removed his jacket and had started flapping it about in a futile attempt to beat out the flames; he had succeeded only in fanning the inferno and setting fire to his own clothing. Ignoring the obvious risk to himself, Barney had grabbed the terrified boy and thrown him headlong into the canal to put out the quickening flames. Ina's screams had then alerted him to the fact that his own jacket was now alight. Worse still, it was now clear that the boy, no longer at risk of burning to death, was unable to swim and was struggling for survival in the dark, oily waters of the canal. Barney hadn't hesitated. Once in the water, he'd known that he too was safe from the flames but he'd also known that the boy was in real danger of drowning. Below the surface of the stagnant water lay many dangers in the form of tangled weeds and household garbage and the steep banks were slippery. Thankfully, Barney had always been a strong swimmer and, despite the boy's struggles, he had been able to drag him to the bank so that Billy and Ina could haul him to safety; the banks were muddy so it hadn't been easy and they'd put themselves in some danger in the process.

Once he'd been sure the boy was safe, Barney had swum the short distance to the road bridge, where he'd been able to pull himself clear by clinging on to the timber struts beneath the bridge; a passing postman had helped him to climb up to safety. Several passers-by had stopped to give him a cheer!

The sound of the approaching fire-engine had been a relief but it had proved to be too late. The flames had taken some time to die down. In the end, almost nothing had been left of Ina and Billy's precious caravan, their much-loved home. Despite the flames and smoke, however, the blackboard of The Wayside Pulpit had stood firm and undamaged with its carefully inscribed message of hope shining out for all to see: "God is Love".

The boy had been rushed to hospital and Barney had been taken alongside him in the "black maria" to receive treatment for burns to his right hand and a knock to his left ankle, the result of contact with the solid timbers of the road bridge. Two ambulances had been delayed by a road accident so the police van had proved to be a convenient alternative. Barney had often seen the maria outside the pubs at closing time, seen the polis loading it up with "customers" when things got out of hand; he'd never expected to be one of those customers himself – but he'd been glad of it.

A crowd had gathered and, before Barney and the injured boy had even reached the hospital, several versions of the incident had already been circulated. The arrival of a polis van had fuelled a great deal of speculation! One version of the events of the day, favoured by some of the more colourful local characters, portrayed Barney as an avenging angel fighting off the forces of evil and throwing one of the protagonists into the canal, where he'd almost drowned. This version had also portrayed the local polis as dragging Barney, hero of the hour, off to languish in the city jail, charged with attempted murder! A good story, but far from the truth!

It had been during the fire brigade's clearing up operation that Colonel McPhee had been passing in his Bentley, his chauffeur at the wheel. In his capacity as a local magistrate, the lads from the prefabs would come to his attention in due course but his immediate concern had been for Billy and Ina. He'd always had a soft spot for "The Reverend" and his wife and had been quick to offer them a helping hand. He had immediately offered them refuge on his estate and the means to get them there. This had been an obvious solution! He'd taken charge! Like Duffy, he was an old soldier, a leader of men, a man of action!

With Alfie perched on Ina's knee, they had been driven to Glenderrin in style. From the back seat of the enormous Bentley, Ina had allowed herself one tearful backward glance towards the smouldering wreckage of their beloved caravan and then she'd dried her eyes and turned her face towards the road ahead. All they had left were the clothes on their backs but they'd had bad times before. They were alive and unhurt, she, Billy and Alfie. There wasn't a fortune in the bank but they did have some savings to help them pick up the pieces and make yet another fresh start. They'd done it before. The most important thing was that they were all alive and they were together!

Billy had told Barney all about their rescue by Colonel McPhee when he'd visited him in hospital. Barney didn't want to talk or even think about what might have happened that morning if he hadn't decided to call on Ina and Billy. They were good people and he'd known that they would help him, that they would help him now when he needed that help most but, after this, they were going to need a great deal of help themselves. It was going to be up to him, up to him and Daniel – but where was Daniel? Where was he?

It was while he was on watch at the front window that Barney noticed the jeep and trailer pulling up next to the entrance to their close. It wasn't a vehicle that he'd ever seen in Abercrombie Terrace before and he was surprised to see three large collies riding in the back. Intrigued, he watched for the driver but didn't recognise the man who climbed down from the driver's seat and stood looking around him as if to get his bearings. Barney saw him pushing his cloth cap to the back of his head before turning to open the passenger door next to the pavement. When Billy stepped out and turned to wave up at the window, Barney knew that it was over, that Daniel was safe, that he'd been found! He suddenly felt tears of relief streaming down his face. On the day of the accident, he hadn't been able to cry, hadn't been able to shed a single tear but now they streamed as if they would never stop.

In the time it took to reach Glenderrin, Gus and Billy told him so much that his head began to spin but through it all he held on to the news that Daniel was with Ina and he was safe. That much was clear and that was the most important thing. Bit by bit, the story would be told and then, when the time was right, and that had to be very soon, he would tell Daniel his story, a story that was long in the telling and sat heavy in his heart, as cold as stone.

He'd tried with all his might that day, tried to stop in time. It had been a through train, an express, taking people to the Highlands north of Crianlarich, where they would be safe from the nightly air-raids that were reducing the town to rubble. The passengers, many of them small children, were to disembark at Crianlarich and board coaches that would take them on to the isolated highland villages where the women and children would be safer than in Riverside with its shipyards and factories. The men went with them but, to their credit, returned to what was left of the town to make sure that the work of building the much-needed ships and tanks went on. Several such trains had been scheduled for that day and extra drivers had been needed. Barney had been an obvious choice!

The train, full of anxious people, was not due to stop along the way and so, by the time it had reached Bankside, the stoker had done his work; the engine had a good head of steam. A local train with very few passengers on board was following behind. It had been the sight of the women racing along the platform towards the oncoming trains that had drawn his attention. They were waving and pointing towards the line. At first, he hadn't been able to work out what was happening and then he'd seen their faces, heard their frantic cries; he'd done all he could but it takes time to stop a train! He'd jumped down even before they'd come to a halt, left the stoker to it, run back along the line, but he'd known, known before he'd reached them that it was too late, that they were gone. He'd seen Walter turn his head just before... He'd turned just long enough for him to know, to see, for a fleeting moment, the face of his only brother cradling a tiny child in his arms.

In one of the last air raids of the war, Daniel's mother and most of their family, had been lost when a stray bomb had lifted a section of the main railway line clean over the rooftops of the council houses that bordered the line. The air raid shelter, where many families huddled together, had been crushed. Daniel, the the sole survivor, had been plucked from the rubble by Barney, himself, who'd been fire-watching that night. He'd dug him out with his own hands. Thankfully, Daniel had been too young to remember much of this with any real clarity. Afterwards, Barney had taken the boy to live with him as if he were his own son, done all he could to make up for all that had been lost but never had he found the courage to tell him about that day, to tell him about the train, to tell him that he had been the driver of the train, the train that had robbed him of a father. Now, as they drew closer to Glenderrin, Barney knew that he would have to find that courage soon before Daniel also heard the sympathetic whisperers on the stairs. But first, just for now, he needed to see Daniel, to know that he was safe and to hear what he had to say.

As they rounded the last bend in the winding lane, the cottages came into view. The driving had been wild and it was a miracle that the three sheepdogs were still in place in the trailer. Barney could only assume that they were well used to travelling at breakneck speed along winding country lanes!

Gus dropped them off in the lane and, with a friendly wave, drove off towards the stable yard. He had to keep his word and check on the ponies and the colonel's horse before heading home. He reckoned, in view of the events of the day, that he'd lock them all up for the night. He wouldn't be wasting any time, however, as the dogs were restless and needing their supper. The evening was drawing in. It had been a long day and a strange one but he had a feeling that it was going to end well. There was no sign of the colonel's two layabouts and he didn't expect to see them again but he was taking no chances; his shotgun was by his side and he was prepared to use it if he had to! Gus smiled to himself. It had been fortunate indeed that he'd called at the polis station to have a quiet word about things and to find out if they had any idea where he might be able to find Billy. Billy had stopped by to see if there was any news about Daniel and was standing right next to the desk in the hallway as he had arrived. Things couldn't have been better!

Barney and Billy watched the truck turning into the stable yard before they closed the garden gate behind them and made their way up the long path that led to the front door of the cottage. There was no sign of life. Billy pushed the door and turned the brass handle but nothing happened.

"Of course," he whispered, "Ina will have locked it. Quite right too in view of what Gus was telling us!"

"We'll knock on the window," ventured Barney, also

keeping his voice low, "or do you think that would scare them?"

"Not sure!" replied Billy softly. "I'll call through the letter-box and let them know it's safe to open up!" "Ina!" he called. "It's Billy. Barney's here with me as well! It's quite safe. It's only us! You can open the door!" And she did!

Chapter 13

An Ending

To the north, the hills were already topped with snow; the first gentle flakes had caught the hedgerows and, up on the moor, the sheep were huddled in the hollows. More snow was on its way. Soon, it would be here. The lower paddock, hard with frost, was empty and silent now apart from one loud and lonely pheasant calling vainly for his mate. The puddles at the edge of the lane and in the ruts were frozen solid as was the water lingering at the bottom of the pails in the stable yard.

Long ago, the swallows had deserted the barn, heading for the warmer climes of Africa, while skeletal trees stretched icy fingers towards a wintry sky. By now, most of the Autumn leaves had stoked the bonfires but some still lay in ragged heaps at the edges of the lane. In the morning light, it was possible to see right across the paddock and beyond. From his vantage point, high in the branches of the chestnut tree, Daniel could see right across the field, over the hedge and into the garden itself, where the piles of logs by the kitchen door were growing higher and wider every day as Glenderrin prepared for the snowstorm that was already promised on the edge of the wind.

The main windows of Glenderrin House had caught the rays of the morning sun, its pale light reaching into every corner, breathing life into the new day. These large, panelled rooms with their high ceilings and open fireplaces had finally proved too much for the colonel's housekeeper, Mrs Atkins, who had, at long last, handed in her notice, packed her bags and gone to live in Ayrshire with her sister, Morag.

However, Mrs O'Callaghan, the colonel's new housekeeper, was already hard at work polishing the wide bay window that looked out on to the rose garden below. This particular spot - this particular window - was reserved for the Christmas tree and, in her mind, she could already see it, its coloured lights glittering in the dark. With so many children and so little room, there had never been a proper Christmas tree in their tiny tenement flat in Abercrombie Terrace, not what she would call a "proper" tree. This year things were going to be different!

"Do just as you like!" the colonel had said. "It will be a treat to have some youngsters about at Christmas! For the first time in years, I am actually looking forward to it!" The fact that his nephew John and his family had moved into nearby Ivy House had also boosted the Christmas spirit.

Mr O'Callaghan, happier than he'd ever been in the shipyard, had pruned the colonel's rose bushes to perfection, closely supervised by Mr Duff, who had made several visits to help with the garden, a garden that had been sadly neglected over the years. Daniel had been pleased to note that Rustler had not accompanied his master on these occasions. Duffy had known for sure that Rustler and sheep would not be a good combination and had sensibly left him at home! With Duffy's help, the garden was returning to its former glory and the colonel's appreciation had known no bounds. Duffy, basking in the glow of this unexpected praise and admiration, was also enjoying the benefits of Mrs O'Callaghan's cooking and had mellowed beyond belief. Mrs O'Callaghan had described him as "a work in progress".

The colonel, a man of action and firm decisions, had rejoiced in the departure of his two worthless farmhands, now safely at the other side of the world in Australia, and had wasted no time in filling all his unexpected vacancies! Grateful to Gus, Daniel and Ina for their timely intervention, he'd been quick to see opportunity in the midst of chaos.

"That's my way!' he'd replied when Uncle Barney had asked him if he was quite sure. "My way! Always has been! Always will be! Actions speak louder than words! No point in hanging around when firm decisions are required!"

When Daniel thought about it, it seemed as if the pieces of a gigantic jigsaw had somehow fallen into place. Life had changed and it was good! For him! For Uncle Barney! For everyone that he cared about! He smiled to himself as he suddenly thought about one change in particular. Mrs O'Callaghan had, at long last, been able to get rid of the fine-tooth comb. The country air had done the trick – that and a foul-smelling shampoo provided by a Mr Gus Ferguson! He'd winked at Daniel when he'd handed the bottle over to Mrs O'Callaghan. Daniel suspected that it was something he normally used on his sheepdogs or perhaps even on his sheep but he was saying nothing about that to Esther! The main thing was that it had worked, much to the relief of Mitchell, the colonel's chauffeur, a man who was very particular about his appearance and who had viewed Joshua's wild head scratching with considerable alarm. Mitchell had kept his distance from the O'Callaghan tribe until he was quite sure that the shampoo had really worked but, in the end, he'd been so impressed by the outcome, that he'd persuaded Gus to let him have some of it for washing down the Bentley!

Disturbed by the ringing of horseshoes in the frosty air, Daniel turned his head in the direction of the lane. Marianne, heading home from her early morning ride, was warmly wrapped against the cold. She looked smaller than usual, perched high on the enormous golden horse, but Daniel knew that she was safe enough.

Midas was a gentle giant. Ears pricked, the horse paused for a moment to survey Daniel in the tree above him. Marianne shortened her reins and the golden horse stood still, his head raised and his bright eyes fixed on the boy high in the branches above him.

"Morning, Daniel!" called Marianne, "See you're up there again! Is your Uncle Barney still over at the stables?" Daniel nodded and grinned. He liked Marianne. She'd promised to teach him to ride when the holidays came round and that would be any day now! According to the colonel, his daughter had been a more frequent visitor to Glenderrin since the arrival of Daniel and Barney; she was spending much more time at the stables now that Uncle Barney was in charge, more time than ever before. Uncle Barney seemed more than happy to have her help and he had a spring in his step that Daniel hadn't noticed before! The colonel had winked knowingly at Daniel when he'd spotted Uncle Barney wearing a rather expensive cashmere scarf – an early Christmas present from Marianne, bought in London during one of her flying visits. Ina and Mrs O'Callaghan were intrigued by the way this friendship was developing! There had been a great deal of whispering and something that Daniel could only describe as "giggling"!

"He's clearing out the stalls," called Daniel, in answer to Marianne's question. "Mr O'Callaghan's giving him a hand. Mr O'Callaghan's getting the loose box ready for Midas." With a wave, Marianne turned Midas towards the yard and his breakfast. The golden horse needed little encouragement. He was ready for home.

Settling himself more comfortably on the branch, Daniel strained to catch a glimpse of any sign of life at the big house. He studied the downstairs windows in particular. Esther should be up and ready by now although she liked to lie in bed a little longer on Saturdays! They all had to be up very early on school days so that they could catch the bus that took them to the high school in the town; the other O'Callaghans were dropped off with the younger children at the primary school in the village. Behaviour on the bus was usually good in the mornings when everybody was still half asleep but could get rather lively on the way home in the afternoons! Esther and Daniel were always the very last to be delivered at the end of the day, by which time the driver had had enough and was ready for his tea!

Most of their friends from Bankside School had transferred to Riverside High, which was good. Looking back, the last few days at Bankside could have been difficult but, after Uncle Barney had explained the whole story to Miss Deacon, she had talked to all the others and had made quite sure that neither Daniel nor Esther would have to face too many questions from anyone.

Really, everyone had been great. Miss Deacon had even explained to all the pupils in Assembly that Percival House was not somewhere to be feared; she had said that children who had lost their families in the war were well cared for there and went to a very good primary school on the other side of the river. She'd said that she knew a lot about it because she'd actually worked there when she'd been a student teacher. All this had made a very positive impression on Esther, who, there and then, in Assembly that morning, had decided that she too would be a teacher when she left school, just like the much-loved Miss Deacon with her endless patience and her beautiful auburn hair. She would specialise in teaching orphans! Since making this decision, she had worked harder than ever at school and was, on a daily basis, amazing her proud mother with her academic achievements! Like Mr Duff, Esther was basking in unexpected glory!

As if reading his thoughts, Esther, herself, suddenly appeared at the window directly below where her mother was still working. The O'Callaghan family now occupied the lower rooms in Glenderrin House where the former housekeeper had lived alone. It was a comfortable self-contained flat with plenty of room for everyone to have a bed of their own; no-one had to sleep '"top-to-tail" any more! "Playing at Sardines" Mr O'Callaghan had called it! Esther was looking in Daniel's direction. He kept waving until Esther saw him and waved back. Even at this distance, he could see that she was smiling. It was going to be a good day.

Most days were good days now. The nights too. The dreams still came from time to time but, for the most part, they were gone. Uncle Barney had told him about the train and he had listened with an aching heart. Afterwards, he'd put his arm around his uncle's shoulders and the cloud that had darkened their days had disappeared never to return. Now, once a month, they went back to the Memorial Garden, taking a bunch of heather from the heather farm and, from time to time, they went back to Abercrombie Terrace. New people lived in their flat now but there was always a warm welcome from old friends and neighbours. The gas lamps were being replaced with tall electric ones that looked more like sculptures than anything else and, at the end of the terrace itself, new flats were to be built for some of the people whose homes had been destroyed in the bombing. Abercrombie Terrace was another "work in progress"!

Mandalay was also going to need work but Uncle Barney could turn his hand to most things. It felt like home already but, with help from Ina, Marianne and Mrs O'Callaghan, who seemed to know about curtains and colours of paint, it could only get better. It was going to take time but with Ina and Billy close by, life was bound to be good. Marianne had told Ina and Billy that they could stay in her cottage for as long as they needed to; she would stay at the big house when she came up from London so there would be no need to worry about finding somewhere else; they could take their time.

"Stay forever, if you like!" she'd said.

As things had turned out, another solution had presented itself in the most unexpected of ways. Mitchell's wife, Diane, had surprised everyone by announcing that a baby Mitchell was on the way and that they would be moving out of the lodge at the end of the lane and into larger premises just across the way. Ina and Billy could have their cottage, which was very smart, and Mitchell would still be on hand for the colonel. Mrs Mitchell had got everything worked out! A smallholding, part of the Glenderrin estate had become available just across the road at the end of the lane. It would provide lots more space for their growing family. Mrs Mitchell had decided that she and Mr Mitchell were going to have lots of children, just like the O'Callaghans, and keep ducks and chickens and sell free range eggs! It had all come as a surprise to everyone, especially the father-to-be, but he was getting used to the idea and, after all, the last few months had been full of surprises all round. It had been a very eventful year at Glenderrin House!

Sadly, although he'd been asked to lead the Christmas service at Glenderrin Parish Church, Billy was still struggling to find a parish of his own but, in the meantime, he'd found some work at Riverside High working as their new German teacher. He was enjoying his work and had proved to be a popular addition to the staff. As a bonus, he was looking forward to being able to afford a proper Christmas present for Ina this year.

Daniel had heard that the boys from the prefabs had found a way to play their part in putting right a great wrong. Following a challenging court experience with Colonel McPhee on the bench, they had willingly agreed to help restore the caravan site by the canal; one of them would always carry the scars of that dreadful day but, nevertheless, had insisted on playing his part. Several weeks had been spent in tidying up the land itself and, thanks to the Romanies of Green Lane, an old caravan had been donated to replace the one that had been lost in the fire. With a few coats of paint and some minor improvements to the interior, it had proved surprisingly comfortable. Mr Morgan and his friends from the garages had kept an eye on progress and had enjoyed giving advice when necessary. Mrs Morgan, keen to be involved, had found a new tenant, a Mr O'Neill. Mrs Morgan was keeping a close eye on him to ensure that he kept the premises tidy and in good repair. Regular checks were to be made by the said Mrs Morgan to make quite certain that the former "Devil" was behaving himself and keeping out of trouble. So far, so good!

An enthusiastic gardener, Mrs Morgan was now organising a garden-improvement scheme for the prefabs. It looked as if, despite the new flats, they were going to be a feature of the town for some time to come and so she was "taking them under her wing". Her team of gardeners included many of the young lads who'd helped with the caravan project and they were keeping her fully occupied while Mr Morgan was at the garage! There would be no back-sliding while Mrs Morgan was in charge!

Ina and Billy had been delighted to learn that their former spot by the bridge had acquired a new resident; their replacement had even taken it upon himself to maintain The Wayside Pulpit on a daily basis, although his knowledge of the scriptures and his handwriting and spelling were never going to rival what had gone before. The current message, scrawled in large letters, read: "Golf Bals FOR SALE – going cheep"!

Esther had scaled the gate rather than taking time to open it and was now heading in his direction. She slowed down as she crossed the field, planting her feet carefully in order to avoid places where the ground was still soft in spite of the frost. She was muffled up and ready! Like Daniel, she knew that Paul would be waiting. It was time to go!

On that unforgettable day when he and Ina had stood frozen to the spot in the hallway of the cottage, listening to the ominous sound of approaching footsteps, it had been with huge relief that they had realised that those footsteps belonged to Billy and Uncle Barney. A nightmare had ended. There had been a great deal of talking and lots of listening as well. Many questions had needed answering.

It was when Ina had asked him where he'd spent the nights that the room had suddenly fallen silent. At first, it had been easy. No-one had been surprised to learn that his first night, Thursday, had been spent in Mr Morgan's garage. That much they had known already. Mr Morgan had found the tell-tale signs of crumbs on the back seat of the Standard and had informed Bob Wishart straight away. Mrs Morgan, who always rode in the back, never ever left crumbs so it had been clear to all that Daniel had passed that way!

It was when he'd begun to explain about meeting Kitty and going to rest in Ivy House that the room had grown cold. Ina, her eyes never leaving Daniel's face, had leaned forward in her chair, anxious not to miss a single word. Billy and Uncle Barney had said nothing but their silence and exchanged glances had spoken of disbelief. Finally, Billy had risen from his armchair to light the lamps and put a match to the logs in the hearth. Unnoticed, the night had gradually settled in.

With hardly a pause for breath, Daniel had recounted all that had happened. His tiredness had left him and he'd felt as if he could go on talking for ever. Now and again, his audience of three had looked at each other and had occasionally interrupted with a question or two but, for the most part, they had listened attentively. He'd told them all about Kitty and how he'd met her on the Meldrum road with her lantern and her dog, Max. He'd told them about her kindness and how she'd taken him in and made him some supper in the warmth and safety of Ivy House, how she'd listened to his story and given him shelter for the night. "Her cottage is practically right next door to Glenderrin House!" Daniel had explained.

"I know!" Ina had said. "Go on!"

Daniel had described Kitty's homely kitchen with its bright fireside. They had all listened intently as he'd told them how she'd talked about her life and how she'd let him sleep on the couch. He'd told them about Kitty and her garden, a garden that was clearly her pride and joy. He'd remembered to mention her husband, Maurice, who'd been a Romany, and her fierce black cat, Mindy! He'd even managed to remember that her grandson, Paul, was helping her with her front garden. He'd remembered everything and they had listened with wide eyes.

"She looked very tired," Daniel had added. "Maybe we could come up to Glenderrin and help her with her garden! I think she'd like that." This suggestion had been directed towards Uncle Barney, who had said nothing. Ina and Billy had exchanged glances but had also remained silent.

"The back garden went back for miles," he'd continued. "There was even a wood at the far end but it was like a jungle. It just seemed to swallow Kitty up! She said that her husband, Maurice, was dead and that she's on her own now. Anyway, I'd like to go back and thank her for helping me. Her grandson, Paul, helps her but there's masses to do so I think she'd like it if we... "

His voice had tailed off. The silence in the room had finally brought him to a stop! In the end, it had been Billy who'd been first to find his voice.

"Did Kitty tell you her surname?" he'd asked.

"No, I don't think she did," Daniel had replied. "She just said to call her 'Kitty'. I didn't ask her second name. Do you know her?" Billy had looked lost for words. Turning to Ina, he'd looked like a man in need of help. When she'd finally spoken, Ina's voice had trembled and in the stillness of the room, Daniel had listened intently, trying to make sense of what she was saying.

"Maurice, Kitty's husband, was Maurice Robert Fairley. Yes, he really was a Romany, who came to Glenderrin House long ago looking for work. He was a handsome young man and something of a charmer. Kitty was a bright and pretty girl, wild and full of fun, a gifted artist too. Yes, Billy and I knew them both. They did run off together, just as she said. It was a long time ago. Before that, Kitty was Kitty McPhee. She was the colonel's sister."

"The colonel's sister! She didn't say anything about that!" Daniel had cried. "So she ran away, a bit like I did - but she came home again – back to Glenderrin!"

"Indeed she did," Ina had continued, "and she did make peace with her family. Maurice was accepted and spent his life working here on the estate; he was well respected and his death two years ago in a road accident was a bitter blow to everyone who knew him and, of course, very hard on Kitty. She did have Max and Mindy but, sadly, they didn't last long after Maurice went and that was the end of things. Kitty was never the same after that and... " There had been a pause that had filled the room.

"But Max and Mindy were with her," cried Daniel, "I saw them!" Ina had looked at Billy, as if seeking inspiration.

"Go on," Billy had prompted. "You're doing fine and Daniel does need to know."

Ina had taken a deep breath, clasped her hands tightly in her lap and continued, "I have to tell you, Daniel, that Kitty Fairley died last summer. No-one seemed to know what was the matter. Most people thought she'd just lost heart. Since then, Ivy House has lain empty."

Daniel had stared, simply stared. Ina's words refused to sink in. Turning to Billy and Uncle Barney, he'd been met with blank looks.

"But she was there," he'd cried in disbelief. "She was real. She helped me. How could that be and why would she do that?"

It had, in the end, been Uncle Barney who'd offered an attempt at an answer. "I don't believe I can say 'how'. That is well beyond me," he'd said, glancing in Billy's direction, "but I may have some idea about 'why'. You were in trouble and Kitty took care of you. She looked after you and made sure that you came to no harm. She talked to you about her life and told you that her grandson, Paul, was helping her with her garden?" Daniel had nodded. Uncle Barney had looked hard at Daniel - had given him time to think.

"That would be Paul Fairley!"

All the time that Daniel had known him, Paul Fairley had walked with a limp. A bout of Polio, when he was a very small boy, had left him handicapped but he was a determined lad and a hard worker, the sort who would gladly help anyone and someone you knew you could trust. Paul's parents had been travellers and when they had decided to leave the high road, they'd had no further need of their old caravan but had been keen to find new owners for it. Parked next to the canal, it had become Ina and Billy's much-loved home.

Paul had had several jobs. Working alongside Uncle Barney at the coal yard had been one of those jobs. He'd spoken to Daniel many times, always kindly, but never once, in all those years, had he mentioned that day - never once! But Daniel had always known that Paul, like Uncle Barney and himself, was a regular visitor to the Memorial Garden in Bankside Park. Once or twice, Daniel had seen him there, just standing quietly on his own. He'd known that Paul was doing what he had done many times; he was reading and rereading the inscription that, alongside the name of Walter Abercrombie, also bore the name of a small boy who'd fallen on to a railway line and never had the chance to grow up... Robert Fairley, aged two years.

Robert Fairley, known to his family as "Bobby", had been Paul's brother. Paul had been there that fateful day, had seen Bobby fall down on to the track and had rushed to save him. Daniel's father had pulled Paul back from the edge of the platform, stopped him from climbing down on to the line before jumping down himself.

It had taken a few moments for Daniel to find his voice. "On the mantelpiece," he said, "there was a photograph. On the back it said 'Granny and her Boys'." Uncle Barney had nodded. "The boys were Paul and Bobby, Kitty and Maurice's grandchildren!"

In the silence that followed, Billy was the first to speak. "Your Dad lost his life trying to help little Bobby but he kept Paul safe. Kitty hadn't forgotten," he said. I think she was repaying a debt. She was keeping you safe.

"Daniel! Daniel!" Esther's voice brought him back to the present.

"Are we going or not? Paul's going to be waiting!"

Climbing down from the tree, Daniel gave Esther a knowing look. He'd been waiting for her arrival for some time but that was nothing unusual. Esther was not the best time-keeper in the world!

"Come on!" he said, with a grin. "We're going to need the cart."

Cutting through the stable yard to pick up the handcart, Daniel called out to let Uncle Barney know that they were on their way. Marianne was helping to fill the hay nets and Mr O'Callaghan was sweeping the yard when Daniel and Esther arrived.

"Make sure you choose well," called Uncle Barney, "and, if the one for Glenderrin House is too big for you to manage, leave it with Paul. Marianne and I will collect it later." Mr O'Callaghan grinned and Esther giggled. Daniel had heard that giggle many times before!

"We'll be fine," he shouted, grabbing hold of Esther's sleeve, "Come on, Esther, hurry up and help me with this cart!"

Paul was waiting by the gate of Ivy House with the huge tree for Glenderrin already trussed up and waiting to be loaded on to the handcart. Mr Fairley and Paul had been cutting trees for the shops since first light.

"It's enormous!" exclaimed Esther. "I hope Mum's got enough lights for this." She had never seen a Christmas tree as big before and couldn't help wondering if it really would fit into the chosen spot by the main window.

Daniel reassured her that it would. "It's going to be just fine," he said firmly. "This tree is going to be just fine! Everything is going to be just fine! This is going to be the best Christmas ever!" and he meant it!

"Would anyone like a mince pie?" Mrs Fairley called from the kitchen. "I've just taken some out of the oven." No-one needed to be asked twice. The kitchen was warm and welcoming, just as Daniel had remembered it but, since Paul and his family had taken up residence, there had, of course, been changes. The furniture was different and there were new curtains at the windows but, on the mantel, a photograph that he recognised remained in pride of place and, on the walls, Kitty's pictures were there for all to see.

Looking through the kitchen window and out into the front garden Daniel could see that, despite the shortening days, Paul and his Dad had worked wonders. Kitty would have been pleased. Beside the shiny, new wrought iron gates a freshly painted sign advertised "Fairley's Heather Farm" and, next to it, a temporary notice announced that Christmas trees were now on sale.

It was warm in the kitchen but their stay had to be brief. Esther and Daniel had two more trees to collect, one for Ina and Billy and one for Mandalay. It was going to be muddy work; they were glad they'd worn their boots.

Years before, Maurice had arranged his little plantation in an orderly fashion so it was an easy matter to find two trees just the right size. Mr Fairley cut them down and helped to load the cart.

"This looks quite a load to me," he said with a smile, observing Esther's nervous expression as she anticipated the return journey to Glenderrin House. "I think Paul had better go with you or there could be a problem!" Esther's smile returned.

While Mr Fairley organised the cart, Paul led Daniel and Esther along the muddy garden path, through the neat lines of fir trees and the vast garden and on towards the thicket beyond.

"I've got something to show you," he called over his shoulder. Keeping a promise made to Kitty, Daniel and Uncle Barney had spent some Saturday afternoons clearing the undergrowth in the wood, helping Paul and his father to cut down some of the brambles that were choking the pathways but they hadn't reached as far as this. Paul and Mr Fairley had made further inroads into new territory.

"Dad and I were working on this yesterday," said Paul. "We had a feeling we'd find them somewhere here." Without saying anything more, he pointed to two small headstones nestling in the shelter of three silver birches...

Esther and Daniel stepped forward together and bent down to read what was carved into the grey stone. Daniel read the first aloud. It was inscribed: "Max, Old and Full of Days". The second stone, exactly like the first, bore a simple message that made him smile: "Mindy, Asleep at Last".

A rustle in the undergrowth beyond the birches, made Daniel lift his head. Just beyond where they were now standing and leading into the wood, he thought he saw fresh paw prints in the soft ground, but he couldn't be sure! To his left, a pigeon clattered in the trees high above them and took flight; a dog barked in the distance and then was still.

"Come on, Esther," said Daniel. "It's time to go home, time to go home and get ready for Christmas!"

As they closed the gate behind them, Daniel noticed that the old sign that had hung precariously by one rusty nail, had now been restored to its former place. It still carried the warning, "BEWARE OF THE CAT!"

About the Author

Robina Cooper now lives in rural Lincolnshire with her husband, Sam, but was born in the West of Scotland and grew up in Clydebank, which was ravaged by the Second World War when the local shipyards became frequent targets of enemy bombing. "The Blitz", as it came to be known, reduced much of the town to rubble and cost many civilian lives. This book is set in the years immediately following the war.

Although the author, did not live through the war itself, she spent a great deal of time listening to the exploits of those who had. Their stories, the challenges they faced and their strength in rebuilding their town and their lives following the conflict provide a backdrop to the writing.

Although the story is fiction and all the characters are fictional characters, the landscape is not unfamiliar to the writer and many years ago there was an accident on the main railway line that passes close to Dalmuir Park, near the town of Clydebank. The brave boy, who tried in vain to rescue a toddler from the track, is remembered on a memorial plaque close to the spot where it happened.

The author used to pass it every day on her way to and from school. However, the incident in the novel is not in any way intended to replicate this tragedy.

The author has just completed her second novel, entitled "The Staircase."